SEA BLUE AND LOVING YOU

CAROLINA COVE SERIES
BOOK 4

KAY LYONS

KINDRED SPIRITS PUBLISHING

"Triple whammy tonight," Sally said with a mutter.

Zoey Barnes continued her approach to the nurses' desk with a nod and traded one file for another once she'd entered the locked area.

The rest of the hospital used tablets to keep track of patient care, but on this floor, they were a safety hazard. Old-fashioned note-taking was deemed less dangerous than walking around with something that could be grabbed, broken, and used for self-harm or as a weapon. "King tide, full moon, *and* the weekend."

"Lord help us all," the desk nurse added with a shake of her curly head and a pleading glance upward.

Zoey noted the woman typed at warp speed, no

doubt transcribing all the notes from the day in an attempt to stay on top of things. "How long have you been here, Sally?"

"Since before Mercie called off.

She must've watched the news before coming in," the woman muttered dryly. "So I'm doing a double and then going home to *sleep* until the cows come home, and if my neighbor pulls out the power tools before I'm through, I just might be in here as a patient. Him, too."

Finished with whatever she logged, Sally lifted her head and stared at Zoey over the top of her glasses.

"You look like crap."

"Wow. Okay," Zoey said with laugh. Sally was as plainspoken as they came, but she was typically more circumspect when it came to doling out observations.

"Said with love, baby girl. You look like you could use a vacation."

"Who needs a vacation when you live at the beach?"

Wilmington, North Carolina, had easy access to multiple beaches and still more beaches within a short drive. People came here to vacation from all over the world.

"Uh-huh. And when was the last time you took a day and actually *went* to the beach?"

Zoey opened her mouth to answer but couldn't.

When had she gone last?

"Exactly," Sally said knowingly. "You need to go —but not tonight."

Feeling the weight of Sally's warning, Zoey sighed. "That doesn't sound good. What's up?"

"You've got one bed open and three downstairs waiting for consults."

One bed and three potential patients? Great.

Zoey lifted her hand and rubbed at her throbbing temple. "Okay. Well, everyone's tucked in and I think it's fairly quiet up here for the moment, so I'll head downstairs now. You know where to find me."

"Yup."

Zoey emptied her hands and swiped her badge before punching in her key code to let herself out of the locked station. She made her way to the secured doors, nodding to the guard there. She repeated her actions and used her badge and code to clear the door and kept going, through another set of locked doors to the elevator beyond.

When working with psychiatric patients, multiple systems were needed to ensure not only their protection but that of the other hospital patients, visitors, and staff. It also made it more difficult for family and friends to get access to the patients needing a break from everyone, especially those closest to them whose well-meaning intentions tended to do more harm than good at times.

The elevator shifted beneath her, and Zoey

leaned her head and shoulders back against the wall, closing her eyes and embracing the momentary silence.

Sally's comment about how she looked hadn't told Zoey anything new. One glance in the mirror in her apartment had revealed the fact her eyes would have to pay extra baggage fees if traveling. The dark circles and puffiness at the corners did nothing to help the lack of color in her face, and when you lived in the south, having *some* tan was a given. Unless, of course, you spent every waking moment locked in the psych ward, trying to help people so they didn't hurt themselves.

She sighed, her entire body aching. Her patients' problems and difficulties ran the gamut, and she wondered how things could be so unfair. Why did life have to be so complicated for some? Problematic? When had people become so cruel toward others? The words they used, the lack of feeling and empathy toward their fellow man? When had everyone become so cold? *Why?*

She opened gritty eyes and stared at the numbers flashing as the elevator descended to the first level. After a full day of her regular patients, she'd grabbed a quick snack and headed to the psych ward for rounds. She and several other doctors managed the patients on the floor, with everyone working an extra night or so a week for on-call consults. Her problem was that on the nights she didn't have rounds, she wound up catching up on her patient files or the daily chores she neglected far too often, which meant she rarely made it to bed before midnight. If then.

All too soon, the elevator dinged, and the parting of the doors brought with it the sounds of a busy Wilmington Friday night.

With the bonus of the moon, tides, and chaos that came with the end of a long week on the Carolina coast, it looked to be a doozy of a night. It wasn't even ten o'clock and she wanted to find a corner to curl up in.

Weekends were the worst. Far too many people numbed themselves to escape their problems. They considered the weekends "free" days, and yet it amplified the stress, pain, and the need for oblivion they tried so hard to escape. Toss in the warm summer weather of June and the influx of tourists and traffic and general chaos, and it was the perfect storm.

"Hey, you."

Logan's deep voice drew her attention to him, and she glanced over her shoulder to find her pseudo cousin and longtime friend somewhat hidden behind a beam.

He smiled when she met his gaze, but she also noted his frown as he took in her appearance. As tired as she felt, she knew she probably looked worse. Yay her. "Don't you have better things to do than stand around for the nurses to ogle?"

Dr. Logan Devoncourt had retired from the military late last summer but still wore his hair high and tight to match the hard hewn body that looked fresh from the exercises of boot camp.

His dark brown hair held a hint of gray along the short sides, and his deep blue eyes were steady and intense as they raked over her. The only non-military thing about him was the scruff on his jawline and chin, but even that he kept neat and trimmed in that fashionable way so popular in magazines.

When he'd first arrived at the hospital, all of the female staff and some of the male scrambled for the chance to work beside him, hoping to catch the eye of "Dr. Hottie." Once they realized Logan wasn't just a pretty face and didn't hesitate to call them out to level up with their work, only the sharpest and most determined continued to try. She'd be curious to see who'd win him in the end.

"Don't you have better things to do on a Friday night than to work nonstop?"

Zoey felt a rush of color rising into her cheeks. Ever since Logan had asked her out and she'd turned him down, things between them had been... different.

Had she read the invitation all wrong? Had he actually asked her out on a *date*—or simply as a friend? To chat and talk about hiring at the hospital?

She should've asked, should've clarified the reason for his request before making an excuse and turning him down. That way they could've avoided this awkwardness and tension that seemed to appear whenever they were in the same vicinity. Maybe she made too much of it, but she definitely picked up on a tension inside him that wasn't there before. Something she couldn't put her finger on. Had he taken her refusal personally? She had to think the man was used to getting whatever he wanted.

Logan shoved away from the wall and moved toward her, not stopping until his six-feet-two-inch frame towered above her four feet and eleven inches of lousy height.

"You feeling okay, Shortstack?"

Irritation bombarded her at the childhood nickname, and she watched as he searched her face. Was she all right? No. People kept trying to hurt themselves.

She shifted her gaze so he couldn't see just how exhausted she felt. Such a simple question asked in a caring tone brought the sting of tears to her eyes... "I'm fine. Here for consults. What do we have?"

Several seconds passed with Logan simply staring her down, but since she refused to let him see more than she wanted, he seemed to catch on to the fact she wasn't going to puddle at his feet or cling to his chest.

She refused to be made to feel less than. She

worked the same demanding schedule as multiple other doctors, and she didn't hear anyone questioning their status.

"Right. Okay, there are two typical. One is a definite admit but the second I'll leave up to you."

"Sounds good."

"And... I don't want you seeing the third one alone."

"Excuse me?" He hadn't just gone all he-man protective on her, had he? Seriously?

"Humor me," he said, though it came out more like an order from a man used to giving them.

Apparently you could take the man out of the military, but you couldn't take the military out of the man. Who did he think he was? "I'm a big girl, Logan. I've got a degree on the wall and everything."

Her words came out sassy and pointed and removed any hint of the vulnerability she'd felt seconds earlier. But something about the way Logan looked at her, like he really could see that insecure girl inside of her, left her squirming in her not-so-beautiful flats.

Zoey shifted her gaze and glanced at the tablet she now held, pressing a series of buttons to pull up the requested consults.

She scanned the notes of each one, noting histories of admittance, blood test results, and the like.

One name she didn't recognize. One she sadly

did. And the other... "Extensive psychiatric issues," she murmured in regard to patient number three.

"And arrests for assault, which is exactly why I don't want you in there alone."

She pointed to a highlighted note. "Says here he's sedated and calm."

"Zoey."

"Logan, don't be ridiculous. I'll be fine."

Zoey glared up at her friend before a nurse walked by and she caught the woman eyeing Logan like the walking man meat he was. Logan didn't seem to notice the woman, but Zoey found it hard to believe he *couldn't have* noticed.

Were the rumors true? Had he really never taken any of the offers shot his way over the last year?

Oh, she knew it was smart not to date where you worked, but she'd even heard the Boardwalk Babes discussing Logan's lack of love life.

During the summers of '58 and '59, four of the prominent Carolina Cove neighbors and friends had given birth to baby girls.

The proud mamas had taken the five girls for daily strolls in their prams—and the locals had nick-named the group the Boardwalk Babes—a name used to this day by the sixty-somethings determined to know every aspect of their children's lives.

The five Babes now had twelve children between them, with the twin Babes, Rayna Jo and Adeline, each having a set of twins of their own. Logan and his identical twin, Michael, were Adeline's sons.

"Humor me," Logan said.

The words were an order and a growl that left her narrowing her gaze on him and fighting off anger that burst from deep in the pit of her belly.

She'd worked in this hospital longer than Logan, and while she might not have his brawn or the five years of extra experience his age and the military provided, she was just as qualified. "Do you doubt my abilities? Because if so, we need to come to an understanding right now. I won't have you under-mining my work or having my colleagues believe I can't handle my job."

Logan looked surprised and then exasperated by her statement.

"No, I don't doubt your capabilities, Zoey. But I know danger when I see it, and the guy in that room..."

"Is a patient, like any other. Thank you for your concern but I'll be fine."

Logan seemed to sense she'd go to battle and this was a fight he wouldn't win.

His lips tightened into a hard line, and he straightened to his full height before giving her a curt nod.

"Keep your guard up."

Anger—or maybe it was disappointment that he

didn't see her as capable—made her lift her chin. "I always do."

She waited, watching as he muttered something under his breath and behind the fist he rubbed over his mouth at the same time before he headed off toward the far end of the ER.

A breath expanded her lungs but gave her no peace.

Great. The last thing she wanted was to fight with Logan, but she couldn't help but be sensitive after working so hard. Far too many people—men, especially—looked at her and found her lacking. They saw a woman under five feet tall and considered her a child due to her stature.

They didn't see the intense studying to pass her exams just like everyone else or the extra time and effort she had to put into *every*thing to be taken seriously by colleagues and patients alike. It wasn't fair, but it was her life, and the chip on her shoulder grew with every comment.

Zoey rolled her shoulders in a poor attempt to release some of the tension making her feel like a puppet on strings. She might have overreacted to Logan's statement due to her fatigue or the tides and the craziness of the weekend, but until she had time to stop and process, she refused to feel guilty about her defense. She'd rallied to her tiptoes and dug in her heels to stand up for herself, and she didn't regret it.

She stretched her shoulders and neck again before she headed down the hallway toward patient one, tapping her fingers against her thigh as she went.

A triple whammy plus a fight with Logan. What was next?

2

Zoey chose to go into the youngest patient's room first and greeted the girl she'd met twice before.

Aya was twelve and had a history of depression, anxiety, and self-harm. She'd cut her wrists. Again.

Zoey checked over the slashes, noting they were not deep enough to do any damage or require stitches, nor did they run wrist to elbow along the vein. The red, painful-looking lines were another cry for help in a world where children were screaming unheard.

Aya stared at the far wall, away from her and the other woman in the room with them. Zoey exchanged a glance with Aya's exhausted-looking grandmother, wondering how close the woman was herself to giving up hope things would change.

"She takes her meds. I give them to her every day and make sure she swallows them."

Zoey nodded at the news and gave the woman a small smile. Taking the meds and leaving them inside long enough to be impactful were different things. And Aya had admitted to bulimia in the past.

It broke Zoey's heart that the girl couldn't see the effect her behavior had on her grandmother. The devastation and weight of her worry were written on her heavily lined face. Grandma was worried—so was Zoey.

Aya couldn't see beyond the moment. Couldn't see the future that awaited her if she'd only hold on and fight through the darkness tormenting her. Every day was a struggle—every minute of every hour as she battled the fears and thoughts that turned the child's brain into a horror movie on replay.

"Fran," Zoey said to Aya's grandmother, "why don't you take a break? Go get some coffee or fresh air?"

The woman knew the drill when it came to assessments and got to her feet. Aya was much more likely to be open about her state of mind and thoughts without her grandmother in the room listening.

Later, Zoey would talk with Fran to get her take on things, but for now, Aya was her concern.

Fran gathered her purse and shuffled her way to

the bed, giving Aya a kiss on the head that the girl didn't acknowledge. Once Fran left the room, Zoey moved closer.

"Aya? What's going on?"

A shrug was the girl's response. But at least it was a response. More than anything, Zoey hated it when a patient—especially a young one—withdrew so far into themselves that they simply didn't care enough about *any*thing to respond.

"Aya," she said a little more firmly, "come on. What happened? What made you hurt yourself again?"

Tears flooded the girl's eyes with shocking quickness given Aya's silent and stoic demeanor, and Zoey steeled herself against the pain now ravaging Aya's sweet face.

Some patients were easier to assess than others. Some kept their emotions locked down, and Zoey didn't instantly connect with them.

But girls—whomever—like Aya? Zoey felt herself get sucked in and swallowed up, and she prayed that, in doing so, she managed to make a difference and ease that burden.

Some people might label her an empath or say that she had a big heart. All she knew was that there were some patients that radiated so much pain and heartbreak that she sometimes felt as though she absorbed it through her skin because of the weight she felt after meeting with them.

"It's stupid," Aya said.

"Nothing is stupid if it makes you want to hurt yourself."

"I— I hate him."

"Who? What happened, Aya?"

The girl's face turned bright red and more tears fell.

"He— We— You know."

"Ah." Twelve and sexually active. Not a good sign.

"But when it was over, he laughed. He said I was s-so pathetic he knew I'd be easy."

Zoey twisted her fingers together in her lap until she felt them turn numb.

"He said... He said he just wanted to do it. And that I was *bad*. He laughed and laughed."

"Oh, Aya..." So many thoughts ran through Zoey's head. The legalities of coercive sex with a minor and then the long and arduous process of proving it. Were there pictures? Videos? "How old was this boy?"

"I dunno. Older than me. I can't believe he told everyone," she said in a low voice.

Stupid, stupid, stupid boy, Zoey thought. "Aya, you know that he's the one in the wrong here, right? That things like that are personal and not meant to be shared?"

Aya sobbed, her shoulders shaking, tears rolling,

but no sound emerged from her. Like the hurt went too deep for it to even have sound.

"*I don't want to be here anymore*," the girl said in a raw voice. "I just want to stop hurting."

The words tore out of the girl's throat, and she curled in on herself, arms folded protectively over her knees as if to make herself as small as she possibly could. To disappear or to hold in the pain to keep from shattering from it.

Zoey tried to focus on the fact that if Aya wanted to be dead, the girl unfortunately knew how to make it happen. It was a sad fact that such knowledge was as simple as a Google search or even from Aya's past stays in the children's psych ward. The patients talked about such things even though they were asked not to and monitored. Whispered conversations happened no matter how diligent the staff tried to be, and stories of how were shared. It was sad how many ways one could harm oneself if they really wanted to. Sadder still how creative some people could be trying to make it happen.

Zoey focused on the fact that Aya hadn't done any of those many *other* things and instead did what she'd done to get her grandmother's attention—which had brought her here, where Aya knew she'd be kept safe from herself.

Zoey talked to Aya for a while longer, letting the girl talk as much as she wanted to about the events leading up to this moment. The twelve years of Aya's life had been fraught with pain and loss, physical abuse, and being taken from her mother's care. When would it get easier?

Once the girl ran out of words, Zoey informed Aya that she was going to be admitted. Aya would be able to safely rest and get counseling while they would try new meds to help her better cope with her depression as well as counseling to deal with the aftermath of what had happened.

Zoey didn't say anything the girl hadn't heard before, but Zoey went over it all according to protocol before calling a nurse to order an anxiety med to calm the girl down while they got her moved upstairs.

Because of her fragile state, Aya would require an aide to stay in the room with her at all times whether or not her grandmother was present. It was the only way to ensure Aya's complete safety.

Zoey finished her notes in the room while the nurse administered the medication. Aya's tears slowed and eventually stopped as the med kicked in. Fran returned, and after Zoey filled her in on the plan, the woman reached down and grabbed a bag and placed it on Aya's bed at her feet.

"I keep it laundered and packed now," the woman whispered, eyes red from tears. "So it's always ready when she has to come."

The reality that the twelve-year-old girl had a psych ward go-bag was not a pleasant one, but it was one far too many parents faced. Clothing had to be ward appropriate. No strings or ties, no belts, no shoelaces. Zoey quickly checked the contents even though it would be checked again upstairs and nodded. "She'll like having her own clothes instead of a hospital gown."

"Dr. Barnes, I don't... I don't know what to do anymore. I don't know how to help her or make her stop."

Zoey swallowed hard at the brokenness in Fran's tone and words and hugged the older woman. When the aide arrived, Zoey turned with Fran and walked the older woman out of Aya's room to make the trip home alone.

The first seventy-two hours, no one was allowed to see Aya. It gave the girl time to calm down and for the med changeover to begin to take effect. It also gave the girl some distance from what had brought her there and the counseling to cope with the aftermath and the future situations she might face.

Fran would return and visit when allowed, but until then, she'd have to use a patient code to check on Aya via phone.

Zoey finished up her notes and inhaled, closing her eyes briefly. She forced herself to clear her mind so she could focus on the next patient. Then the next.

This young woman was twenty-one. The cops had brought her in after she caused a disturbance at a bar and assaulted another person. She'd then threatened to kill herself. Cassie had several cuts that needed stitched up on her cheek, but after talking with Cassie, Zoey realized the woman wasn't suicidal at all but thought a stay in the ward meant she wouldn't go to jail. Cassie begged Zoey to keep her there at the hospital, but Zoey couldn't sign off on that request, not with every bed full and more cases to assess as the night—the weekend —wore on.

Once Cassie was cleaned up and her minor injuries seen to, the young woman would be taken and processed by the police.

An hour or so after her conversation with Logan, Zoey came to the third patient in C-11. She rapped softly on the door before pushing it open, and the man's gaze fastened on Zoey the moment she stepped into the room. A chill ran down her spine when she stared into his seemingly black gaze.

Shakespeare said the eyes were the window to the soul, and a glance into this man's eyes revealed a darkness that could only be described as severely ill.

Logan's warning came to mind, but she reminded herself of the man's sedated condition. He was awake but under control. EMS had given him enough of a dose to make sure of that.

She forced a smile and braced herself for whatever the next assessment would bring.

She'd heard it all. Very little could shock her at

this point. But it didn't make the listening any easier. "Hi, there. I'm Dr. Barnes."

Patients like the young ladies she'd treated were one thing. They were troubled or emotionally immature or attempted to work the system to their advantage.

But others...

Exhaustion filled her and dragged at her very soul. Every so often, she came to a person so lost inside their mind that they wore their evil thoughts on their faces, and she sometimes feared getting sucked into the void because the darkness was so strong. "Mr. Smith, do you know where you are?"

"Hospital..."

"That's right," she said softly, nodding. "Can you tell me what happened that brought you here?"

"Sister."

He made the word sound sinister with the utterly bitter way he spat it. "Your sister?"

"She thinks I'm crazy."

Zoey broke eye contact and stared down at the tablet she held. "It says here your first name is Kevin. May I call you Kevin?"

He nodded, his beady black eyes following her every move until Zoey glanced down yet again to regather her thoughts.

"Well, Kevin, I'm here to help sort this out, okay? Will you tell me what happened?"

Zoey moved to the rolling stool provided in every

room and made herself as comfortable as she could get under the circumstances. "How was your day? Did you have breakfast? Remember what you had for lunch?"

The questions weren't so much about his nutrition, though that was definitely a factor, but about positioning him in the day and then letting it play out. To see where or how or what had changed to make a man require EMS to sedate him in order to control.

"I want to leave."

"I know. But I'm afraid you can't go home just yet. Not until we figure out what's going on that scared your sister so badly she called for help. Do you remember what happened?"

Zoey reread the notes taken by EMS and the ER nurse who'd logged him in and gotten his vitals. Kevin lived with his sister. Seemed to be hallucinating. Talking to imaginary people. Was not violent at that point but "talking crazy." EMS sedated to help calm.

"You think I'm crazy, too."

She looked up and forced herself to meet Kevin's dark gaze. "I don't like that word, Kevin," she murmured, settling back on the stool. "I think during the bad times in our lives, we need help, and sometimes we don't know how to ask for it, so people —friends and family—have to do it for us. It's as simple as that."

"I want to leave."

"Kevin, I know you're upset with the situation. I don't blame you. No one does. But we have to deal with what's happened. Who were you talking to when your sister called 911?"

His nostrils flared and he stared in her direction. Not *at* her but just beyond. Zoey fought the urge to look over her shoulder because she knew no one was there. Kevin saw someone, however. That much was apparent.

"*No.*"

"The sooner you talk to me the sooner we can work on getting you out of here."

He glanced back at her, then his gaze shifted up once more. Zoey watched as he shook his head and a deep flush took over his face and neck. "*What did she do?*"

The voice behind the question was so ominous she knew he said it to whomever he saw, either about her or the sister who had sent him here. Zoey's stomach pinched and she uncrossed her legs to stand. "Kevin, I'm sorry. I just remembered something I was supposed to do for a previous patient, and I need to run to the nurses' station. You rest for a bit and I'll be right back," she said. "We'll continue the assessment in just a minute."

Zoey rose to her feet, and as she did so a blur caught her by surprise. She couldn't believe the man moved so fast. She'd just straightened from the stool when he sprang off the bed, blanket and all, and grabbed the tablet out of her hold, swinging it and clipping her in the face above her temple.

She fell sideways over the rolling stool and down with a jarring thud. Pain shot up her arm when she automatically tried to catch herself, and her head banged against the floor from the momentum. Stars sparked in front of her eyes in a flash of white and the haze of red.

The stool crashed into something, bounced off and back into her legs, and she flinched and ducked down even more when something struck her again.

She blinked but couldn't see anything due to her eyes burning and the tears that flooded them from the sting.

Seconds passed. Long seconds of shock and horror and that immediate replay of images in her mind trying to process how she'd come to be on the floor. In pain. Bleeding?

She heard swearing and then—

"Zoey."

3

She recognized Logan's voice but the blood scorching her eyes completely blinded her. She blinked and kept blinking, squeezing her eyes shut and then reopening them, but nothing worked to clear her vision.

Her mind spun, the room whirling like a carnival ride. Strong arms wrapped around her and swept her up, the move making her mind spin even more.

The scent of Logan's cologne teased her senses, but it also made her feel sick as nausea rolled over her.

People shouted. Someone screamed.

She pressed her head against Logan's shoulder to try to still the bombardment to her senses as he carried her somewhere. She wasn't sure where. She thought he took her out of the room but—

"He's got a knife!"

"*Security!*"

Logan cursed under his breath and picked up speed as an alarm sounded and she forced herself to focus on the words.

Code Silver. Armed and combative patient.

Zoey felt herself getting squeezed between Logan and a door as he shoved it open, felt the whoosh of air on her bloody-wet skin as he carried her inside and whirled around to make sure it shut behind them. She was pretty sure she heard the loud click as the hospital went on lockdown.

"Don't move," he ordered.

Logan sat her down on the floor. Still blinded, she felt for the hem of her shirt and shakily raised it to try to wipe some of the blood away. Every beat of her heart was a pulsating pain in her head.

"Here. Let me."

Logan's large hand gently grasped her chin before sliding along her jawline to tilt her head back.

She flinched when something wet touched her forehead, the moisture running down her nose and off the tip. After a few more swipes and wipes, Logan grasped her hand in one of his to press her fingers to her head.

"Hold that tight. Can you see now?"

She blinked a few times. The sting was still there though not as bad as before. Her eyes watered like a faucet on full blast, but she nodded, able to take in

Logan's blurry masculine visage a scant inch from her own.

"You'd better believe I'm going to say I told you so," he growled.

She grimaced at the warning, his tone, and even though she knew she owed him an apology, she wasn't quite ready to admit defeat at the moment. So she said nothing, the hand holding the bandage to her head growing heavy. "Pick a better day if you do," she muttered. "Today is *not* the day."

Logan inhaled and sighed deeply, his minty breath hitting her face. "Thank God for sarcasm. And lucky for you, it's not too bad a cut," he said in his best doctor voice. "Head wounds always bleed excessively, but I think a stitch or two along your hairline should take care of it. Keep pressure on it and keep those eyes open."

She nodded once but instantly regretted the action when the movement made the pain worsen. The adrenaline faded as shock began to take hold.

She leaned her head back against the wall behind her, grateful for the support since it was the only thing keeping her upright at the moment.

"Tell me what happened," he said. *Ordered.* But she understood the urgency and upset in his tone, especially after the warning he'd issued before she'd gone in for the consults.

Zoey forced her lashes up and watched as he searched the boxes and bins along the shelves of the supply closet, using the time to recall the incident that had gotten them here. "One minute he was on the bed, and the next, he wasn't."

Logan knelt in front of her once more and, ascertaining the bleeding was over, opened a suturing kit.

The alarms continued to sound the code silver, echoing the painful throbbing skewering her skull.

Logan murmured something under his breath. "I can't find numbing cream."

"It's fine."

"This is going to hurt, Zoey."

"It already does. Just do it. I can handle two stitches."

"If you say so."

Her breath hissed out of her at the flash of pain when the antiseptic hit the open wound.

"You dizzy? Double vision?"

She opened her eyes and blinked at him. "Yeah. Just get it over with, please."

While she held her breath and gritted her teeth —which did not help her head—he quickly stitched the cut at her hairline. He bandaged it next before he pulled a penlight from his coat pocket.

She groaned when he flashed it in her eyes. "Seriously?"

"You have a concussion. How many fingers?"

She glared at him despite the pain it caused. "Forty-five."

"Zo."

She ignored his bad mood. "Two?"

"You asking or telling me?"

"Both?"

He made a frustrated sound.

"Keep those eyes open."

With the cut taken care of, he buried his big hands in her hair and gently felt her head for lumps. She closed her eyes again because it felt so good when he tenderly massaged a few tension-tight spots, but she gasped when he hit a painful bump. "Ow."

He leaned forward to check it out and then pressed a swift kiss to her forehead.

"Sorry."

The low rumble of his voice and the sweet sentiment jarred her eyelids up, and his gaze was right in front of her. He blurred before sliding back into focus, but in that brief second, she thought she saw something in his gaze. A flash of... something more?

Long seconds passed with them just looking at one another until he cleared his throat.

"Zoey, you have to stay awake. Talk to me. Tell me exactly what happened," Logan ordered.

She focused on the incident, forcing herself to concentrate. "I-I... I knew I'd have to find him a room and shuffle someone around upstairs. He was in the bed. I stood up to leave and suddenly he wasn't in the bed anymore. He moved so fast. Then he grabbed the tablet out of my hands and hit me with it," she said, lifting her fingers to the bandage. "Then I fell. I fell over the stool. I think that's when I hit my head."

Logan's expression darkened even more. He stretched out a hand and pulled her fingers away from the bandage, holding on to them after he'd lowered her hand to her lap.

"Did he touch you again?"

"No. I... I don't think so. It happened so fast. He threw or dropped the tablet on me and ran out of the room, I think? I couldn't see because of the blood."

He'd paused in his examination as though needing a moment to calm himself at the words, but he continued soon after.

His hands slid from her head, down her neck, and then over her shoulders, pressing gently as he checked for injuries.

She sucked in a sharp breath when Logan made it to her arm and he stopped his exam once more.

"You going to take it off or am I going to cut the sleeve?"

Color rushed into her face even though she wasn't sure why. He'd seen her in a bathing suit all of her life whenever their families got together on the beach. This was a medical emergency.

So why did the thought of the two of them alone and her wearing just her bra feel so weird now? Especially since it covered more than most bathing suits. "Just cut it. My shirt is ruined anyway."

He grabbed hold of her sleeve and ripped the cotton peasant blouse with one yank.

He whistled softly at the darkening bruises along her elbow and gently moved her right arm through various motions, checking its flexibility.

"You're going to be colorful for a while. Undoubtedly sprained. I don't think it's broken, but you're definitely going to feel that over the next week or so. We'll have to get a couple of scans to be sure, but if everything checks out, you should be fine with a sling for a few days until the worst of it is over."

"It's fine. I don't need tests."

"We'll need to check your head, too, Zo. Might as well get the complete picture."

"It's just a cut. I'm fine. You're freaking out over nothing."

"You're concussed. And if you could see yourself right now, you'd know why I'm a bit freaked out."

"But—"

"Stop arguing. You know what the hospital is going to say about checking you out after a patient incident. Resign yourself to it now, because you're going to get a thorough physical before you're allowed to leave the premises."

She groaned, not wanting the fuss but knowing there was no way around it due to hospital protocols. But she was fine. Really.

"Any pain? Discomfort anywhere else?"

"No, just bruises, I think, where I fell. My hip is aching and, no, I'm not going to show you. It's from where I landed."

His big hands gently wrapped around her hips, fingers pressing to check for worse things than bruises. "I think you're right, but the scans will let us know for certain. Are you still light-headed?"

She reluctantly nodded. She hated to admit just how badly her head spun from the blow.

"Stay put," he ordered, getting to his feet once more.

4

Logan moved toward the door, but seeing as how it didn't have a window, he could do nothing but press his ear near the panel and listen.

"Anything?" she asked after a moment.

"No. All quiet."

Zoey lifted her hand to her sore and rapidly stiffening neck and dreaded the next twenty-four to forty-eight hours, knowing they'd be the worst as far as pain went. Her elbow throbbed in rhythm with her aching head, and the overhead lights in the room left her squeezing her eyes closed to block it out.

"I'll try to find you some blankets. Make you a bed."

"I'm fine."

"You're not. I appreciate you trying to pretend but it's useless, Zoey."

She used her left hand and managed to roll onto her knees, then shoved herself up using a hand along the wall, her head whirling and body screaming.

"What are you doing?" he asked as he rushed to her side to steady her when she immediately started tilting sideways.

"I'm okay."

"Sit down. You shouldn't be moving around until we get you checked out. You know the drill."

She shook her head and moved her feet toward the door, aware of the fact Logan was the one keeping her upright. "I'm fine. And I can't stay in here. I have patients and—"

"You're kidding me, right?"

"I need to get out of here, Logan. See if I can help calm Kevin down so he isn't hurt."

"You're not going anywhere," he said, gently holding her upper arms and turning her back to where she'd sat leaning against the wall. "This is beyond your job description at the moment. It's not safe so let security do their job. It shouldn't take long."

She pulled at her blood-coated blouse and winced when her hand came away red. That was *a lot* of blood. "I really liked this shirt."

A huff left him. "We'll find you another one."

"Okay, but I still can't stay here. I need to change before I check on my other patients. They'll freak out if they see all the blood."

"Right now the most important thing is keeping you and everyone else safe. Come on. Let's sit you down, and then I'll see if I can find a gown or scrub top for you to change into. There's got to be something in here."

"Logan?"

"What?"

"I can't... I have to... I can't breathe."

At her words, Logan immediately forced her down to the floor. Once down, his fingers found her pulse.

"What's going on? Talk to me, Zoey."

"I can't..." Every inhalation required an insane amount of force. Her head throbbed, her elbow and arm and hip ached like nothing had for a very long time, but now her chest felt like something squeezed her in a vice. "I feel like I'm dying," she whispered, using her injured arm to clutch at her chest and throat.

"Zo? Hey, sweetheart. Focus on me," he said. "I think you're having a panic attack. Have you had them before?"

A panic attack? Seriously? She was a counselor, for pity's sake. A doctor. This wasn't funny. "No. I don't think so." But the symptoms matched, and she was definitely getting a taste of what so many of her patients suffered.

"Listen to me, okay? Listen to the sound of my voice. Focus on it and slow your breathing. Breathe in for five counts, hold for two," he said. "Now out for seven counts. Good. You're okay. You hear me? I'm right here and I won't let anything happen to you. Breathe in, five counts..."

A shrill sound made her scrunch her face up from the pain it caused, and it took several seconds to realize it had come from her.

"*Zoey*."

She heard more than a bit of stress in his voice. "What's happening to me?"

"Adrenaline and shock. *Breathe*. Come on, sweetheart, focus on my voice. Breathe in. Hold. Release. Now do it again. Take a breath."

She used her good hand and clawed at his arm, trying to use him for support to get up only to be gathered up into his arms. Cradled against him so tightly she wasn't sure if that was the reason she couldn't breathe.

"I've got you. Sweetheart, look at me."

She sucked for air like a fish out of water, her good hand clutching his arm like a lifeline. She breathed in, held, out. Over and over again.

Logan palmed her cheek, lifting until he forced her to look at him. He ran his thumb over her cheekbone, back and forth, timing his breathing to match hers. His face blurred for a moment and went fuzzy, but whether it was due to blood or tears or panic, she wasn't sure.

His fingers found her pulse again. "You're doing great. Keep going. That's it."

Logan kept talking. Encouraging her and softly stroking her face whenever he wasn't monitoring her pulse. The weighted pressure of his arms securely around her helped as well, and she told herself she needed to have more of her patients using weighted blankets as part of their routine.

Adrenaline had taken over, taking her post-incident reaction to a whole other level of shaking, but thankfully it felt like the vise around her chest had started to ease. Almost as though Logan absorbed it into himself.

"That's right. Slow and easy. I'm here. I've got you. Okay? I've got you. Listen to my voice. Focus on being right here, right now."

She unclenched her fist from his shirt and placed it over his wrist, holding on to the strength and warmth and grounding he offered.

"Slow and easy," he said again, his lips brushing her forehead. "That's good. Match my breaths."

Several minutes passed with them frozen like that, his lips to her forehead, her good hand gripping his wrist so tightly she felt his pulse, or hers, both, beating in rhythm together.

After another moment, Logan kissed her hair.

"Hey, do you remember when we were teens and we went jet skiing? That time Jack spotted all of those girls partying on an island and went to talk to them only to realize they were three times his age?"

She smiled at the memory of her then twenty-year-old older brother thinking he'd hit the jackpot of hot young things to flirt with. Instead he'd found a moms' weekend of empty-nesting mothers and grandmothers.

A huff of a laugh left her, and she couldn't help but feel the tenderness of Logan's calloused thumbs brushing over her cheek, gently whisking away the tears left behind from her earlier episode. "He was so embarrassed."

Logan's chuckle warmed her insides, his dark blue gaze holding hers. "They thought he was their prize, though. They barely let him leave."

She giggled, remembering the way they'd catcalled her brother and teased him. Which then made all of the cousins rib him until Jack had finally said enough and taken a swim to get away from everyone.

"What about when we went to the south end and got stuck? How Jack came to rescue us but then got stuck trying to pull us out."

"And then the tow truck got stuck." She smiled but also groaned. "We were grounded for *weeks*."

"Grounded but together so we still had fun."

She nodded. They had. When she thought of her

childhood compared to that of her clients, she recognized just how blessed and terrific it was. She hadn't been abused nor neglected. And she had a built-in friend system that had protected her back all through school, which meant bullying was never a problem. Not once everyone realized the group of pseudo cousins ran as a pack.

The fond memories and Logan's hold took her breathing down to normal, but she still had the overwhelming need to get out of there. To rush upstairs to check on her patients and make sure they were okay.

Lockdowns were scary. The sirens and noise, the inevitable controlled chaos of staff rushing to get into position.

Zoey squeezed Logan's wrist tighter and forced herself to open her eyes. "Shouldn't they have caught him by now?"

"You know the drill, Zoey. They have to make sure everything is secure. We'll be free as soon as the alarm stops."

"But what if he went into Aya's room? She's only twelve." The moment the thought registered, Zoey let go of him and attempted to scramble to her feet once more. Logan stopped her, his muscled arms wrapping around her in a gentle but unbreakable hold.

"They'd already taken her upstairs. I saw her being transported."

"Really? I should go—"

"*Stop.*"

"But what if—"

"You're hurt, you're not thinking straight, and from the feel of you, you're pulled tighter than a drum and in shock. The hospital has protocols in place, and right now we're going to follow them. You are going to sit here and let me take care of you. So shut up and let me."

She felt his lips brush over her head, taking the sting out of his order, and felt him gently running his hand up and down her upper arm, careful not to hit her injury but holding her in place all the same.

The hand on her uninjured hip didn't move, and he kept a firm grip as though ready to stop any further attempt she might take to make a run for it.

The alarm continued to sound, every shrill shriek grating on her last nerve. An hour or more passed. Maybe less. Maybe more?

She lost track of how long they were stuck in the room, but she leaned against Logan's hard body while hers throbbed with pain. The faster her adrenaline faded, the more sore and stiff and exhausted she felt, like her body locked up and all the moisture had been sucked from her interior, leaving her brittle and tired and worn. Fight-or-flight response. She knew what it was, but until now, she hadn't really experienced anything so intense. Yet another thing that would help her with her patients' care.

Way to think positive, her muddled mind mused.

Finally the alarm stopped and the silence was so abrupt it was deafening. Then she felt Logan's gaze on her and they exchanged a look.

"Don't move."

"You give way too many orders," she muttered.

"Only when they're needed."

Logan extracted himself from beneath her and set her on the floor as though she were made of glass. He got up and went to the door, testing to see if it was unlocked. It was and he yanked it open and took a look outside before returning and swooping her up in his arms.

"Logan, no. I can walk!"

"Hush. Stop being so stubborn."

Stubborn? He was calling her stubborn?

He carried her out and set her in the first available bed, calling orders for tests and scans despite her protests. She saw several wide-eyed nurses taking in her bloody blouse before they went into action. When one of their own was hurt, the hive swarmed.

No one would heed her protests, and she was whisked away, with Logan walking quickly beside the gurney as she was taken to Imaging. The only time Logan left her was during the tests, and even then, he was in the next room with the technician, watching and waiting for the results.

Once the tests were finally completed, the

hospital administrator appeared in the doorway along with a policeman, both of them asking questions and getting her statement for official reports.

Logan was right in that her arm wasn't broken but severely sprained. It was now wrapped and placed in a sling, and the painkillers they'd given her had taken effect and lessened the throbbing, leaving her pleasantly drowsy.

"Good thing you have a hard head," Logan murmured, staring at the images on the portable screen even though the neurologist had already cleared her.

"I have to agree. But you still get the next week off," the administrator said, giving her a stern look.

"What? No," she argued. "I'll be fine in a few days. I'm sure I'll be back to work by Monday at the latest."

"A week," the man said again. "I don't want to see you here for any reason, got it?"

"But my patients—"

"They'll be covered," the older man ordered. "Same as they would be on your days off. You rest and heal and come back fresh."

"We have your number if we have any more questions," the police officer said. "But we should be good to go. You got lucky tonight, miss. This could've been a lot worse with his history of assault."

She didn't want to acknowledge the truth of the statement, especially with Logan standing there as one too-tall I-told-you-so. "I realize that. Thank you. But that doesn't mean I need a week off."

"Enjoy the vacation and do not let me find out you didn't follow orders," the administrator said in a no-nonsense tone. "Do you have a ride home?"

"She does," Logan said before she could answer.

"I can drive."

"Not concussed," Logan said, arms crossed over his chest as he stared her down.

She huffed in aggravation, and Logan and the other man exchanged a look before the man shook his head.

"Good luck."

The administrator and policeman left, and Logan moved toward her with determined steps.

"You don't have to see me home, you know. Your shift is over, and I know you don't want to wait around until the release paperwork is done. I'll be fine."

He ignored her.

"Fine, I won't drive. I'll get an Uber."

He leaned over the bed and braced his arms on either side of her. "Listen to me very carefully. You? Aren't getting out of my sight."

Logan hadn't planned a trip to the mountains with Zoey. Though now that he had driven them across the state, he wasn't sorry.

His only intention had been to take her home and stay with her to check on her concussed state, but once they were in his truck, a thought had occurred and wouldn't let go. Hours later, they'd almost made it to his cabin.

Logan glanced over to where Zoey sat in the passenger seat and resisted the urge to take her hand in his. The last thing he wanted was to wake her up before they got there. So long as she slept, she wouldn't realize they were no longer in Wilmington —or that he hadn't taken her home to Carolina Cove.

After a dose of pain relievers and something to

help calm her nerves, he'd escorted her out of the hospital and lifted her into his truck, leaning her seat back a bit for comfort and fastening her in tight.

He'd started for home and the apartment she shared with her sister, Lily. Lily was a travel nurse currently working in California, so she wasn't there to keep an eye on Zoey, but after a few red lights and some pondering, he'd found himself coming to a decision and purposefully driving slowly. This gave plenty of time for the exhaustion of the night to kick in along with the meds.

With luck, Zoey would sleep the whole way there. If not, he'd have to come up with a quick plan B.

The powerful engine and music from the radio added to the peacefulness of the ride.

It took a solid five to six hours to get to the mountains from the coast, and he really didn't want to have to argue with her if she came to and decided to protest. Because he wasn't driving them back. Not even if it meant bungee-cording her to her seat until they arrived.

If that's what it took... maybe he had a plan B after all.

Logan glanced over at her again, taking in Zoey's delicate beauty. She had the girl-next-door look about her, which probably helped when it came to her patients opening up to her. It was also something he'd always found himself drawn to.

A million freckles dotted her nose, cheeks, and forehead, and her brown hair floated around her shoulders in soft, curly waves.

She hated being short. Hated being called cute because of her height-challenged frame. But he loved her snack-size body, and he had to watch himself when they were all together on the beach and she was in a bathing suit because it was so hard to take his eyes off of her.

His Zoey loved action films and was a total James Bond fan, loved the color teal and the oatmeal chocolate chip cookies his mom made. If only she wouldn't take on so much of her patients' problems. He could see it in the strain on her face, the dark circles under her eyes. The way her short but stacked framed had slimmed from missing more than a few meals.

Zoey's panic attack in the supply closet had confirmed his suspicions. Maybe it had been brought on by the attack, but he couldn't help but think it exacerbated a problem that was already there.

His girl burned the candle at both ends and had for a long time, since before he'd returned to Carolina Cove and begun working at the same hospital. As much as she took care of other people, she needed someone to take care of her. And while he knew she'd never see him as more than a friend, he intended to do whatever it took to help her get back on track.

Another hour and a half passed, but thankfully he'd filled up the gas tank before work yesterday and didn't have to stop along the way.

Logan focused on the road in front of him, seeing the night sky beginning to lighten as dawn approached.

By the time she'd been released, it was the wee hours of the morning, but thankfully that had worked to his advantage. Between her injuries, fatigue, and emotionally exhausted state, the meds had given him the time he needed to whisk her away. The only problem would be her lack of clothing and personal items. He was sure to hear about that, but considering it was just the two of them, she'd be fine wearing some of the T-shirts and shorts he left at the cabin for spur-of-the-moment trips.

He glanced over at her once again, and his gaze landed on the adorable tilt of her freckled nose. He wanted to kiss that nose. And every single freckle.

The thought made him remember how he'd held her in the supply closet, the scent of her shampoo in his nose, the feel of her skin against his lips when he'd kissed her forehead. She probably thought he was being brotherly, but knowing he couldn't cross the line was the only thing keeping his lips on her forehead and not on her mouth considering the scare she'd given him.

He didn't remember a time when he didn't love Zoey in some way. As a little sister, a friend. Then more than a friend. Sometime during his teenage years and then during his career in the military, he'd found himself corresponding with Zoey more than his other "boardwalk cousins." Maybe it was just her nature. The way she sensed his loneliness in being away from home for so long, like she sought to keep him up to date as though he was present and wouldn't be left in the dark and out of the loop about the goings-on when he did finally make it back to Carolina Cove.

With every letter, she'd revealed herself. Her softness and heart. Her passion and beautiful mind. Their letters had never gotten explicitly personal, never gotten intimate in the sexting type of way. But her letters had meant more to him than she would ever know. They'd carried him through times when he'd felt the never-ending groans of a world where war and pain and injuries occurred far too often and in very dark ways. When he was tired and questioning his life choices.

But since working at the hospital, he'd noticed the same heaviness in Zoey. How her expression remained tense and furrowed whenever he spotted her. It was another reason he felt that he had to take care of her the way she had taken care of him.

One look told him she teetered on the edge of

the cliff. He knew it, recognized it. And he wasn't going to let her fall.

By the end of the five-hour-plus drive, fatigue pulled at his senses. The turn up the mountain left her stirring, and he winced, resisting the urge to floor it in an attempt to get them there and parked before she woke up enough to begin the battle he knew he faced.

Instead, he slowed a bit so the truck wouldn't bounce so much as lightly rock when it hit dips and bumps and drove the twisting, curving mountain road with care.

Another turn left him facing the gate that blocked access to his property, and he pressed the remote button for it to open, slowing so that he wouldn't have to stop and start again and chance jarring her.

He'd contacted his neighbor, Will, before they'd made it out of Wilmington last night and asked the man for a huge favor. Like him, Will was retired military, and when Logan had bought the place a year or so ago, he'd learned Will's brother actually owned the security company where Zoey's brother, Jack, worked. It had made for one of those small-world moments that had linked them as neighbors on yet another level beyond the fact they'd both served.

He and Will weren't best buds by any means since Will tended to keep to himself, but whenever

Logan visited, he made a point to invite Will over for a steak and a few beers out by the fire.

Logan drove slowly to make sure the gate closed properly behind the truck and then continued on up to the cabin a couple of miles away from the entrance.

He exhaled as he rolled to a stop, relief pouring through him after a long stretch of work, the adrenaline rush of Zoey's close call and injuries, and then the drive. He was dead tired, but he didn't dare close his eyes when she would undoubtedly wake up soon.

Logan pressed the button to lower the windows and made sure the cool mountain breeze would be enough to keep Zoey from overheating as the sun rose.

With one last look at her sleeping form, he opened the truck door and got out, careful not to slam it so that maybe, hopefully, he could get things opened up and aired out before she woke.

There was no sign of anyone at the cabin, but when he unlocked the door and went inside, he saw bananas and bread and nonperishables on the counter. Despite the early hour, Will had already come and gone.

Logan walked over to the fridge and opened the door, nodding to himself. He owed his buddy for doing this.

Per request, Will had picked up several days'

worth of food so that Logan wouldn't have to leave the mountain or Zoey. Until she settled in and realized he wasn't going to budge on her taking the administrative-ordered injury leave, he didn't want to risk her being alone or taking her with him into town only for her to attempt to get a ride or flight back to Wilmington.

Speaking of which… He hurried back to the truck and carefully grabbed the purse next to her on the seat, carrying it with him to hide for the time being. He turned off her phone so it wouldn't make a noise or vibrate and then tucked it back into the folds.

The cabin's mantel had a secret hinged top and made for the perfect hiding place to store valuables. It would also be overlooked if Zoey tried to find her purse to make her escape.

That done, Logan grabbed eggs and bacon from the fridge, a fresh tomato, and toast and set out to have breakfast ready for when she woke up.

He'd just finished plating the eggs when he heard a frustrated-sounding shriek quickly followed by a low groan of pain.

Rolling his eyes upward, he said, "Help me out here, Big Guy, okay?"

"Logan? *Logan!*"

He'd purposely left the front door of the cabin open and heard her footfalls as she made her way up the steps. Her shadow blocked the sunlight from filtering into the living area, and he popped a bit of bacon in his mouth before setting her plate on the countertop. "Good timing, sunshine. Breakfast is served. Have a seat."

"Are you *kidding* me?"

The blaze in her pained gaze revealed the firecracker ready to blow, no matter the damage it would do to her hurting body. "What would you like to drink? I have coffee, juice, some sodas."

"Where are we?"

"My place," he said, staring into the fridge at the items available. "I think juice would be best."

"Oh, really? You know what you can do with your juice?"

He grinned as he faced her with the container in hand. "Now, now. You've got to be hungry. Have a seat."

The glare she sent him left him fighting back another smile. She was beautiful on a normal day. Mad? She was flat-out adorable in a sexy, angry fairy or elf kind of way. Apparently he had a thing for that. Who knew?

The thought made him grin yet again, but he was quick to hide it with a hand and a cough when he caught her glaring at him.

"Seriously? That's it? Breakfast and juice? That's all you have to say?"

"It's going to get cold."

"What are we *doing* here?" She lifted her unin-jured arm and waved a hand toward the door.

"There are mountains outside, and the last time I checked there are no mountains in Carolina Cove!"

"Hmm." He leaned down as though to peer out the open window. "You're right."

"*Logan.*"

"Zoey."

"Give me the keys. I'm going home."

She marched up to him and stood toe-to-toe, his size thirteens looking ridiculous compared to her fairy-sized feet. "I'm afraid I can't do that."

"Why not?"

"Because you are in no condition to drive and we are staying here."

"What— For how long?"

He lifted his hand and gently chucked it under her chin, tilting her face and checking her pupils. He was well able to see the pain in her eyes from the concussion headache she tried to ignore as she blus-tered at him. "You have a week off, so...a week."

"A week?"

"That's what I said."

"Well, you can unsay it, because we are going home. Right now. Got it?"

6

"N o. We aren't," Logan said just as firmly.

She was going to kill him. Slowly. Painfully. With her own bare hands—er, hand, as the case might be.

Zoey glared at the unfazed man standing in front of her and forced herself to stay upright instead of curling up on the couch at her right and whimpering the way she felt like doing. It was an effort to stay on her aching feet, pain shooting down her hip and arm and head like lightning bolts. "Where are we?" The words emerged tight, ground out between her clenched teeth.

When her head throbbed worse at the tension, she forced herself to unlock her jaw and take a breath in the hope that it would lessen the painful stabbing in her brain.

"My place—my cabin. I told you about it."

His cabin—in the mountains? "Six *hours*? You drove us all the way across the state and... You *kidnapped* me!"

"That's a pretty strong word."

"What other word describes it?" She shook her head, her entire body trembling with a combination of fatigue, pain, and anger.

"You should sit down. Here, I've got some pain meds for you. You're overdue for them."

"You want to drug me again?"

"I didn't drug you. The hospital drugged you." He winked at her. "I just took us for a drive so that I can take care of a friend."

"And during the drive you didn't think about the fact I don't *want* to be here? Take me home."

She watched as he grimaced and made a face.

"It occurred to me a time or two that you might not like it, but I knew what would happen if you had a week off in Carolina Cove. Zoey, you're trying to ignore the fact you could have died last night."

"Is your driving that bad?" she asked dryly, deliberately misinterpreting his statement. She cradled her injured arm with her good one and tried to think of a way to reason with him. Her headache was getting worse by the second, and she had to think her addiction to coffee and the caffeine it provided was part of the cause. "We'll eat breakfast," she said, "and then you'll take me home. Is there coffee?"

"Yes... but I can't do that."

"Can't or won't?"

"Does it really matter?"

"*Why*?"

"Because I took an oath to care for patients, and right now you're my patient."

"I'm no such thing." Why couldn't he get it through his thick skull?

"You are now."

"*Logan.*" She watched as he turned and moved toward the fridge, his broad shoulders and back taking up a lot of space in the tiny kitchen area.

"We aren't leaving, Zo. You have a week off and you need to heal. What better place than here?"

"My apartment?"

He stared at her from over the fridge door, giving her a knowing look.

"You and I both know, if we were home, you'd be trying to sneak your way back into the hospital to check on patients."

It was true. But what good doctor didn't check on their patients? "So? It's not like you wouldn't do the same thing."

Her uninjured hand fisted so hard her short nails dug into her palm. How could he do this? Just... keep her here? "You can't kidnap me and bring me here. It's... it's unreasonable."

He grabbed the plastic jug of her favorite coffee creamer—he remembered?—and set it on the counter in front of her before moving to pour her a hefty cup. Once that was done, he slid the mug in front of her and pulled up a stool to seat himself at the bar, his plate piled high with food.

"Looks like I already did."

Seconds passed as his words sank in, and it took a moment before she stomped toward the tiny island. After two stomps, she had to lighten the force due to her pounding head and sore body. She felt like she'd been hit by a semi, because there wasn't a single part of her body that didn't hurt. And waking up alone in a truck outside an unfamiliar cabin in the middle of the woods had shocked her like something from a horror movie. If she hadn't known she was in Logan's truck, she would've thought she'd been kidnapped for real.

"Zo, sit down before you fall down. Have some breakfast, drink your coffee-flavored cream, and then we'll figure out what we're doing on our first day here. Yeah?"

Like she had a choice?

Considering the pain she felt and the lure of the two pain relievers sitting beside her plate, she gave him her best glare and watched as he unsuccessfully tried to bank the amusement in his tired gaze.

Only then did she realize he'd driven all night. She'd been released in the wee hours of the morning, and add a six-hour drive to that... While she'd slept in the truck, he'd driven them here. Then fixed breakfast? "What about you?"

"What about me?"

"You're so concerned about me recovering, but when was the last time you slept?"

"I wasn't attacked last night. Don't try turning it around on me."

"It couldn't have been safe driving all this way when you're tired."

"We're here now. Now sit down and eat."

"Or what? You can't kidnap me again."

This time the smile that warmed his eyes caused a flutter in her belly. He really could hide his amusement at her expense better. It had always irked her that if Logan was around whenever she got angry or upset over something, he watched with this look... *that* look on his face.

And now it spiked her anger even more—which did nothing for her head.

Her stomach rumbled out a complaint, and even though she didn't want to humor him, she closed the distance and clumsily hiked herself up onto a stool. She felt light-headed and more than a little dizzy, and while she was hungry, she also had the urge to go back to sleep.

Her mother had always said she was a horrible patient as a kid. Now was no different.

She shakily poured creamer into her coffee. Using her left hand took some serious concentration, but after a moment, she was able to get a good grip on the mug and took a soul-restoring sip. After two more, she set it down long enough to snag the pills and downed them with another drink.

"Good girl. That should help with the pain. Now eat up. If it's too cold, I can warm it up in the microwave for you."

She ignored the praise and the kindness despite her sour mood and picked up her fork with her left hand. It was a struggle to stab a bit of scrambled egg because the fluffy egg kept falling off the fork. Finally she fisted the stupid utensil and managed to stab a bite, but just when she leaned over her plate to put it in her mouth, it plopped to the plate once again. Yeah, being unable to use her dominant hand sucked.

"Want me to feed you?"

The question left her staring up at him with wide eyes and her fork fist tightened. *Feed* her? "I've got it."

She wasn't sure why the thought of Logan oh so carefully lifting the fork to her lips and waiting while she accepted the bite seemed so intimate. Too intimate for what they were. But it did. And that just felt weird.

He tried to pluck the fork from her fist and they waged a silent battle of tug-of-war. Finally he let go and held his hands up before setting his elbows on either side of his plate and clasping his hands in front of his mouth while he watched her.

Okay, so maybe she was overreacting a bit out of

her stubbornness, but if Logan fed her, she'd never be able to live it down.

Zoey glared for a moment before attempting another stab with her fork and lifted it in triumph before opening her mouth and bringing it toward her—where it fell off the fork and landed on her lap.

Logan's loud chuckle left her face burning with embarrassment, and she tossed the fork down with a clatter and used her fingers to pick up the egg on her lap. She set it beside her plate and then picked up a piece of toast already buttered with jelly, carrying it to her lips. "Finger food," she muttered around the bite.

Logan grasped his cup from the table and took a long sip, his gaze holding hers even though she wanted to look away.

"You *are* a stubborn woman," he said finally, gaze sparkling despite his fatigue. "Use your fingers on the eggs, too. It's just us and you need the protein." She munched on the toast, unwilling to admit it tasted heavenly. Her last real meal had been... breakfast yesterday? "You're still not getting away with this," she said, mumbling the words around her food.

"Mmm. Hate to tell you, Zo... I already have."

7

Michael Devoncourt frowned when he pulled into Logan's extra parking space outside his apartment building, noting the fact Logan's designated space to his left was empty.

He checked his watch. Maybe Logan had to run an errand?

Michael had a key to his brother's apartment and could make himself at home while he waited on his twin to appear for their scheduled meeting.

He grabbed the house plans he'd completed for Logan's remodel of a home in Carolina Cove and exited his Wrangler.

The apartment building wasn't the best, nor was it in the best neighborhood, but Michael knew Logan didn't pay any attention to such things when his goal had simply been to be close to the hospital to save himself the hassle of Wilmington's bumper-to-bumper traffic.

He wondered if Logan had considered that once he moved to the island? His doctor brother would have to make a point of adding in quite a buffer of travel time.

Michael made his way up the flight of stairs and down the hallway to Logan's door.

He heard a frustrated-sounding shriek from across the hall, the noise muffled by the door between.

Michael let himself into the apartment and noted the closed curtains over the balcony doors. Apparently Logan hadn't been home today?

He tossed the rolled and boxed plans onto the kitchen island and moved through the darkened apartment to the patio doors. Dust flew when he opened the drapes to the blazing sunlight outside, but light filled the living room/kitchen combo.

Michael had scheduled Logan's meeting for his day off, knowing Logan had done the same. Afterwards they'd planned on grabbing some lunch and heading out on the boat for some fun.

Michael moved to Logan's recliner and made himself at home, sinking into the luxurious leather with a tired sigh since it was rare he found himself with nothing to do but wait.

Michael had just closed his eyes when a frantic knock sounded at the door.

"Logan?"

The woman sounded desperate.

Michael sprang to his feet and closed the distance in four long strides.

He opened the door and a woman quickly shoved a toddler into his arms.

"He didn't show up. *Again*," she growled, eyes down as she sorted through the baby bags she carried. "And I'm already thirty minutes late. I'm so sorry to do this to you, but you said to bring Axl over any time you're here and... I have to go. I'll make it up to you somehow," she said, tossing the bags to the floor inside. "Axl, be good, baby," she said, standing on tiptoe to press a kiss to the kid's cheek. "I'll be back as soon as my shift is over and call you later to check in."

"Whoa... Wait a—"

"Food, snacks, and drinks are in the blue bag. Pull-ups and toys in the other. Thank you, thank you, *thank you*," she said, rushing out the door as quickly as she'd rushed in.

Michael tucked the kid to his chest and hustled after the mother, but the outside door to the building was already closing behind her by the time he made it to the top of the stairs.

Downstairs, he watched as she literally ran across the parking lot and jumped into an old Toyota, peeling out of the parking space like a NASCAR driver.

Michael looked down at the boy staring up at him, his bright green eyes surrounded by a mass of black curls. "Uh, okay, then. Has your mama always been crazy or is this new?"

The kid didn't answer other than to lift his hands to his mouth and slobber on them.

"I guess it's just you and me... Axl? That's your name? Axl?"

"Lolo?"

The kid's confusion couldn't have been more apparent what with his scrunched-up face, head tilt, and frowning expression. Suddenly Axl's eyes filled with tears and his mouth opened on a growing wail when the kid seemed to figure out for certain Logan wasn't the one holding him.

Michael grimaced and carried the kid back up the stairs to the apartment before he could erupt in a neighbor-noticing, police-dialing tantrum. He didn't want to get his mama into trouble, and it was obvious Logan had helped her out before. "Hey, it'll be okay. Your buddy'll be here soon. Want to see what's in your bags? Where's your toys, huh?"

The boy's mom had tucked quite a few things into the bag, and Michael dumped them all out and tossed them to the floor before setting him down. "You like to play cars? Let's play."

He pulled his phone from his pocket on the way down to the floor and sent Logan a text.

Where are you? Your neighbor just thrust a kid into

my arms thinking I was you and bolted. Looks like you're on kid duty today.

Minutes passed but then his phone chimed.

At my cabin. Forgot @ meeting. Gemma is a sweetheart. Be nice. Take care of Axl. He's pretty easygoing.

Wait, what?

Michael stared at the text for a long moment and then blinked as though he'd somehow hallucinated the response.

Seriously? Take care of Axl?

He didn't know the first thing about kids. Caring for them, babysitting them. The last time he'd ever watched over a kid was when he was a kid and his younger "cousins" were around. Even then there were a boatload of other people keeping an eye out as well.

Are you serious?

Gemma needs the hours so let her work. Play with Axl, feed him, put him down for a nap around one.

Oh, is that all?

She wouldn't have brought him unless she's desperate. You can do this.

Could he, though? He didn't even know this woman, and yet somehow he'd wound up responsible for her child.

Michael ran a hand over his head and rubbed hard once he got to his neck. The kid just stood there staring at him with wary eyes, no doubt sensing the problem with this situation.

Michael sighed and tossed the phone down. Apparently his day off was now going to be spent babysitting.

"Lolo?"

Michael sighed and shook his head with a tight smile. "No, little man, you're right. I'm not Lol—Logan. I'm Michael," he said, bringing his one hand to his chest. "I'm... Lolo's brother." Like the kid would understand the concept of twins or brothers. He didn't know how else to explain things, though. "Can you say Michael?"

"'Ikle," the kid repeated, the word followed by a shuddering breath.

The kid was adorable with his mass of short curls, and had Michael not been so gobsmacked by his insanely beautiful mama, maybe he would've actually been able to unglue his tongue from the roof of his mouth and clarify the situation before she'd made a run for it.

He shut his thoughts down in an instant. He had a rule and he wasn't going to break it.

It didn't matter how hot she was or if she was single. She had toddling baggage to care for, and that meant her time wasn't her own.

Michael remembered her rattled rush of an explanation mentioning her presumedly ex-boyfriend or husband ditching the kid. The drama of hostile parenting added to Michael's dislike of the situation. He worked eighty-hour weeks more often than not, and the last thing he wanted was this sort of complication.

While on the one hand, he'd like more info on Logan's beautiful neighbor, he also knew better than to ask. He didn't want Logan thinking she'd sparked his interest when that wasn't the case. Was he curious because of this sudden development? Sure. But it had nothing to do with more than general interest in the boy's mama and this odd situation of mistaken identity.

Michael lowered himself to the floor with his back against the couch, eyeing the kid as warily as Axl eyed him.

"So... guess it's just you and me, kid. What'll we do first?"

8

As Logan suspected, a full stomach and pain meds led to a sleepy Zoey. She'd finally stopped her painful-looking pacing after she'd eaten and carefully lowered herself to the couch to continue her tirade about him supposedly "kidnapping" her, but after a while, the words emerged a little slower, the sentences a little more sporadic, and by the time he finished cleaning up the kitchen, he'd turned to find her sound asleep, her head propped on her left hand,.

He left her that way for a while, letting her settle into a deeper slumber before quietly going over and lifting her feet onto the couch. He smiled at the fact they didn't touch the floor so getting them onto the couch wasn't a big move.

She shifted automatically to get comfortable,

and he waited until she'd settled with her face tucked into a pillow before grabbing a blanket off the bed and covering her with it.

She needed rest. Deep rest that would allow her body to heal and her anxiety level to lower. To come out of fight-or-flight mode and settle back to normal.

Logan propped himself on the edge of the lift-top coffee table and stared down at her for a while. Loving the fact he could focus on her instead of his driving or the million other distractions that came with the modern world or the fact they were "only friends."

After a few minutes, he forced himself to his feet and left the cabin, knowing he needed to call and check on Michael and Axl before allowing himself to catch a few z's.

He'd helped his neighbor, Gemma, out a time or two when her louse of an ex ditched his responsibilities and left her in the lurch. She didn't take advantage of the kindness because usually her mom was able to babysit when needed. But every now and again, Gemma's mom would have appointments or plans that couldn't be changed, and the daycare Gemma used would be at capacity so... he'd offered to help whenever he could.

It was the least he could do for a fellow soldier, and Gemma's four years had qualified her as a sister-in-arms.

Since Axl seemed to like having a man around, they would hang out while Gemma was at work. The kid rarely cried, and Logan had found himself thinking about the time when he'd be watching his own kids.

At least, he hoped it would happen sometime soon. It was all a part of his plan. Retire from the military, get a job at the hospital, get a house, and settle in. Then a wife... kids?

He hadn't wanted to put a wife through the constant moves the military required, so he'd kept things casual all these years.

But he was ready. More than ready. If only someone other than Zoey would come along and distract him from his "friend," because it was apparent she had no interest in him at all.

Logan pressed the button for his brother's cell, and it rang three times before Michael picked up.

"You on your way back yet?"

Logan chuckled at the question and earned a groan in response. "You've got this. He's a good kid."

"He can tell I'm not you and it's weirding him out. And how long have you and his hot mama kept things on the down low?"

Hot mama? Gemma was a pretty woman, but with his broken radar, the woman sleeping inside his cabin was the only one he noticed these days. "We're just neighbors. Gemma was a grunt and now a chef, so I take full advantage of designer food in exchange for helping her out every now and again."

"Chef, huh?"

"Yeah, her ex owns the restaurant where she works but he'll never win father of the year."

"So I gathered," Michael said.

"Sounds like you two are doing okay?"

"So far," he agreed. "We haven't faced the whole eating or napping thing yet, though."

"Just feed him then sit with him on the couch with cartoons. He'll be out like a light." It had worked for Zoey given her injured state, and he couldn't help but think a tired toddler would be five times more susceptible.

"If you say so."

"Give me a call if you have a problem."

"Yeah. Will do. Hey, what's with the sudden trip to the mountains?" Michael asked before Logan could end the call.

Logan filled his twin in on the happenings last night, adding a rundown of Zoey's injuries.

"But she'll be okay?" Michael asked, his tone as angry as Logan had felt due to Zoey being family.

"Yeah, she will be. I knew she'd sneak back into the hospital if she was in town, and I had a few things to check on here, so I decided to kill two birds and all that. This way I can keep an eye on her injuries and she's forced to recuperate. For a counselor, she's very high-strung."

Michael laughed at the description. "Yeah, I don't see Zo relaxing. That one's wound tight. Type A all the way."

Logan felt guilty for discussing Zoey when she wasn't around to defend herself. "Maybe the forced vacation will help remind her to take care of herself, too."

"So you going to tell her?"

"Tell her what?"

"Come on, Logan, seriously? That you're *into* her? That you've always been into her— That you love her?"

He'd been very careful not to let his feelings show when it came to Zoey and his family. Michael included. "I don't know what you're—"

"Deny it all you want, brother, but I see the way you watch her."

"That makes me sound like a stalker."

"Just stating facts. When she's around, you go into La-la Land."

"I brought her up here to help her, Mikey. Nothing more than that."

"Okay, okay. I get it. But you know that pact we all took as teenagers to not date doesn't exist anymore, right? Devon and Oz are back together, and Hadley and Bryson are together now, too."

"That last one doesn't count. No one knew who Bryson was until recently, *and* he didn't grow up with us and wasn't part of the pact," Logan said, rehashing history his mind still couldn't quite comprehend.

Of all the Babes to have a secret baby, he wouldn't have suspected it to be Mary Elizabeth Shipley. Bryson had grown up to be a quality man, however, and Logan much preferred Bryson to Hadley's lying, cheating narc of an ex. They'd all known the guy could be a jerk, but had they known what took place behind closed doors, he knew the family would've dragged her out of there sooner and not let her spend twenty-plus years with the man.

"All I'm saying is that no one would blame you if you tried to make the current situation work to your advantage," Michael said, bringing them back to the topic. "Axl, hey, no— I gotta go."

The phone clicked in Logan's ear, and he laughed, well able to picture Michael hustling after the toddler and whatever mischief the boy had gotten into. Served Michael right for giving Logan such a hard time.

Michael's words stayed with him, though. Of all the people in Logan's life, his twin *would* be the most likely to notice his fascination with a certain petite brunette, but Logan still felt their childhood connection worked against them when it came to romance.

Zoey had known him her whole life. Had known him when he was a pimply-faced teen, heard him fart to get laughs, had witnessed all of his awkward girl-chasing-crash-and-burn mistakes, and worse yet, had undoubtedly heard of his track record during his wilder years when he discovered women loved men in uniform—and a doctor to boot?

No matter how much he tried to keep his private life private over the years, he knew things had been shared that he probably would've rather had kept secret.

He moved back onto the porch and quietly let himself into the house. Zoey slept on, so he grabbed a drink from the fridge and headed out to the porch once again, careful not to let the screen door slam.

He turned with the bottle almost to his lips when he paused, staring out at his mountaintop getaway.

There was just something about this place. Something peaceful and serene. No traffic noise, no bumper-to-bumper traffic. Just the birds and the grasshoppers and an occasional dove.

The sound of the wind through the lush treetops reminded him of the waves hitting the shore, and he inhaled to savor the smell of whatever bloomed naturally around him.

It smelled like jasmine, but he wasn't sure the plant would survive at this altitude when the winters could get harsh. Maybe honeysuckle?

He'd finished his drink and was about to go in to lie down on the bed when he heard Zoey mutter and let out a frustrated sound.

Two seconds later, the screen door slammed and

she appeared in four feet, eleven and three-quarter inches of pissed-off fury.

"Let's go."

Even though the bottle was empty, he tilted it to his lips and pretended to take a last drink, making her wait for his response. "Pardon?"

"You heard me. Let's go. Logan, you can't keep me here and I insist you take me home."

"Ah, see, that's a problem. Because as your doctor, I insist you take a break. You falling asleep in there like that just proves how much you need to rest and recuperate," he said. "So how about instead of fighting me all week, you focus on that? Grab a book and go relax in the hammock," he said, lifting his chin toward it. "Sit here and listen to the birds. When you're up to it, I'll show you the waterfall. Maybe we can even go kayaking one day when you're not so sore."

"All *week*?" she demanded, zeroing in on the time and nothing else. "Logan, I want to go *home*. I want my own bed. I need clothes," she said, plucking at the hospital-issued scrub top she'd put on after her imaging was completed. "I can't stay here. What could I possibly do all week?"

"Nothing. That's the point. As for clothes, I'll find you some," he said, standing to tower over her.

He couldn't help it, he liked the way she stared up at him and scrunched her nose up to combat the glare of the sun. It just fell onto the long list of things he liked about her. "The bed is brand-new and extremely comfortable, and by the end of the week, you won't even want to leave."

A low growl left her, and had he not heard the sound for himself, he wouldn't believe it came from her. He couldn't hide his grin, which made her flare her eyes and make a fist. Ferocious little thing.

"You wanna bet?"

9

Zoey knew she'd been had. And right now, Logan's determination to keep her hostage in his impossibly small cabin seemed like something out of a dark romance novel—but without all the kink.

She understood his concern for her. She'd be concerned if he had been the one to get hurt, but to take things as far as this?

No, this was too much. Ridiculous! He should have taken her home. Maybe slept on her couch for a night to check on her since her sister, Lily, currently travel nursed out of town but... not this.

She remained on the porch while he went inside, and she fell into her automatic stress response of pacing. Her entire body felt pummeled by the fall she'd taken yesterday, but the more she moved, the less it seemed to hurt. At least until she stopped and then everything throbbed.

His porch took twenty-seven paces to cross its length, and once she tired of retracing her path, she moved down the steps and ignored the low throb of her head. The meds Logan had given her before she ate had kicked in and taken the edge off, but she still felt like she'd gone to battle and lost.

The hammock swung lightly back and forth in the breeze, and even though she didn't intend to make use of it, she walked in that direction, hoping to see the neighbor's house. A roadway in the distance. Something or someone who might be able to get her out of there.

She explored the yard a bit but didn't go beyond it since her flats and scrub pants weren't exactly hiking material or snake proof.

As the sun rose in the sky and the temps warmed, she headed back to the shaded porch and settled into one of the rocking chairs, pushing the chair in motion before sliding back into the seat since her feet didn't reach the porch floor.

She wasn't sure when he'd done it, but Logan had apparently come to check on her and left a sealed Yeti with a drink iced down inside it and another dose of pain reliever.

She grabbed the meds and the drink and went back and forth between scooting forward to push the rocking chair into motion and settling back to enjoy it until it stopped rocking. She probably looked ridiculous, but such was par for the course when it came to being short.

After fifteen or twenty minutes, the meds kicked in and the low throb lessened once again to a mere twinge of pain. Her body aches decreased as well, and she pretended to rock her way back to Wilmington since Logan refused to take her himself.

Tomorrow, she thought as she closed her eyes and leaned her head back against the seat.

If she felt better tomorrow, she might be tempted to tackle the long, twisting driveway she'd spied on her walk. Maybe she could wave someone down at the roadway and use their phone to—

Realizing she hadn't even given thought to her purse *or* cell phone—proof of how badly she had been out of it—she jumped up much too fast, inducing a raging head rush, and stumbled down the steps toward the truck.

At some point Logan had locked the doors, but a quick glance inside revealed the tote bag she used as a purse that had been retrieved while she was receiving hospital care was missing.

What the... So now he wasn't just a kidnapper but a thief?

She growled out her frustration and slapped her hand against the scorching-hot door and turned to see Logan oh so nonchalantly leaning his tall, broad-shouldered frame against the vertical porch posts, filling the space to preposterous proportions. He looked a bit tousled, like he'd been napping inside, and it took effort not to notice his sleep-drowsy features. "Where is it?"

"What?"

"You know good and well what. My purse? My cell phone? Where are they?"

"Inside. Lunch is ready. Come and eat."

"Stop trying to feed me and tell me where my stuff is!"

"I just did. Your purse is inside—minus a few key items. Now stop shouting like that or your headache will come back. Don't worry, your belongings are safe."

"Safe *where*?"

"Just safe. You don't need them right now."

"Oh, I beg to differ," she said, closing the distance between them and marching up the stairs. Her head barely met the height of his crossed arms over his chest, and she fisted her hands so tight in frustration that pain shot up her injured arm. "I want my things—all of them—now."

"Nope."

"Logan, you have to be reasonable! You can't keep me here against my will. What about my mom? She'll worry when she doesn't hear from me."

"Tessa got a text from you stating you'd be out of touch for a week's vacation with a friend. She said to have fun and be careful," he told her in a droll voice.

Have fun? Be careful?

She wanted to clobber Logan!

"Where is my phone?" she asked, enunciating each word between clenched teeth. "I have things I need to keep track of, Logan."

"You're not calling the hospital."

"Of course I am! I have patients to monitor and—"

"And you are on paid administrative leave due to an injury at work. You were told to stay away, and like it or not, I plan to make sure that happens. Your patients are covered and you know it."

"I hate you."

He grinned at her words and shook his head. "No, you don't, sweetheart. You know I'm doing this for you. Now come on, let's eat."

"I'm not hungry."

Without warning, he uncrossed his arms and leaned down, wrapped one around her waist, and pulled her in like an octopus. Yup, that was the description she was going with. An octopus that was too big and too strong for his own good. How were the women of the world supposed to react to such caveman-like tactics?

He let the screen door bang shut behind them and carried her to the kitchen, not letting go until he had placed her on a stool at the island.

"You're ridiculous."

"And you're too stubborn for your own good. There's your bag."

She eyed the item she would've sworn hadn't been there when she'd left the house earlier. Maybe she'd missed it? "You are taking way too many liberties, mister."

He laughed at her statement—laughed!—and went to the counter by the sink where two plates sat covered with paper towels.

She dug into her bag but her wallet and cell were both missing. Ugh!

"Avocado BLT on gluten-free toast," he said, presenting the plate to her with a flourish.

"How can you possibly have gluten-free bread? How can you have *groceries*? How long did I sleep?"

He straddled his stool on the other side and settled in before pushing a glass of what looked to be freshly made lemonade in front of her. Seriously?

"I typically order ahead with the grocery store here and pick up on my way up the mountain. So I just repeated an order, added a few things, and called a buddy and asked if he'd get it and bring it up due to the circumstances."

"He *knows* you kidnapped me?"

"He knows I'm caring for an injured colleague," Logan said with a look of exasperation.

She stared down at the sandwich and gave in to the temptation to take a bite. He'd even cut the bread into four triangles to make it easier for her to handle.

Pretty nice gesture for a kidnapper. "I guess I should just be thankful there isn't a red room or a basement."

"Would you like that?"

She'd said it as a joke, but his question left her choking on the bite she'd just taken. Sweat broke out over her forehead and neck, and she could feel the flush heating her up like a lightning strike.

"Talk about learning something new about you," Logan said, his voice taking on a husky note she hadn't heard before. "Interesting."

"Stop it. You know that's not what I... Stop."

"Oh, no. Your blush says it all, sweetheart."

"My blush says you took something out of context, twisted it, and are now... Stop it," she ordered again, so hot she wanted to melt into the floor. She enjoyed reading sexy books as much as the next girl, but she didn't go around talking about them.

Silence fell between them, but a quick glance at Logan proved he still studied her, a look on his face she couldn't quite name—or maybe didn't want to.

Because she knew better. Many a friendship was destroyed by friends letting things lead to more when there wasn't enough between them to sustain it. Resentment built and built until the inevitable implosion, and then they wound up seeking counseling from her.

It was a story as old as time. It didn't matter the age or the gender. It just disintegrated and left the shells of the people behind, hurting and aching and never the same again because they couldn't go back to being just friends.

She picked at the piece of avocado that fell to the plate from between the bread and kept her gaze low.

"Zo, talk to me."

She felt tears prickle her eyes and blamed exhaustion and pain and the overall stress of getting attacked by a patient. "I want you to take me home."

"I know you do. But I think if you give this a shot, you could really enjoy yourself and get rid of whatever's pulling your shoulders up to your ears."

She forcibly lowered her shoulders and realized he was right. Still didn't make it better, though. "I'm not the only doctor stressed out about my patients. You know that, right?"

"I do. But you are the only one I care enough about to make sure you don't self-combust. I know burnout when I see it."

"I'm not burnt out," she said, taking immediate offense. Being tired wasn't burnout.

And okay, so maybe she was a bit more than tired but wasn't that the norm these days?

"Maybe not yet but you're hanging by a thread. It's as plain as day to me."

"One, you *don't* know that, and two, do you really think bringing me up here and not letting me leave is *helping* my stress level?"

He stretched out a hand and gently knuckled her chin up.

"If I took you back and something happened to you because you're not a hundred percent, I'd never forgive myself."

"I'm not your responsibility."

"You are."

"Since when?"

"Since forever," he growled. "Now eat your sandwich."

10

Michael wasn't sure what woke him, but the moment he opened his eyes, he knew he wasn't alone—and that wasn't because of the toddler cuddled against him.

He wiped a hand over his eyes and blinked, only then seeing Gemma quietly moving around in Logan's kitchen.

He'd turned off all the lights but the one in there to help the boy settle in for sleep, and now he watched as his mama removed containers from two large bags. She winced when one of the bags rattled and glanced up at him.

"Sorry, I didn't mean to wake you. I brought dinner if it's not too late? There's prime rib, garlic mashed potatoes, rolls, and lots more. And that chocolate seven-layer cake you like so much."

His stomach growled loudly at the mention of

food, and he looked down before gently extracting himself from beside the sleeping boy. He made sure Axl was comfortable and didn't wake. "That sounds great."

Axl had eaten off and on all day, meals and snacks provided by his mother, but Logan's fridge was decidedly empty when it came to food, and Michael hadn't gotten around to ordering a pizza before the kid insisted he sit with him to watch cartoons. With the kid asleep and his phone across the room, he'd given up the idea of having more than a few handfuls of nuts and a half of a sandwich left behind in the fridge. Thankfully the sandwich was dated, so he knew he hadn't risked his life by eating it.

Michael straightened from the couch and turned only to find Gemma staring at him, mouth slightly open. "Something wrong?"

"Are you sick? Your voice sounds... different."

Michael winced, only then remembering the fact that she'd mistaken him for his brother. "Uh, no. I'm not sick. Look, don't freak out when I tell you this but—"

"What? Freak out *why*?"

"I'm Michael."

"Excuse me?" she asked, her expression going blank.

"I'm Logan's twin."

She slapped her hands over her mouth to

smother a gasp, eyes as wide as saucers as she looked from Michael to Axl and back again.

"It's okay," he said, lifting his hands in a placating gesture, trying to gauge whether or not she was the dramatic type that would start screaming and get the neighbors' attention.

"Please say this is a joke."

He winced. "I'm sorry but it's not."

"Oh my—" she said, hissing the words in a low high voice to keep from waking her son. "Are you saying I was in such a hurry I left my son with a *stranger* and didn't even notice?"

He grimaced at the way her legs seemed to wobble, and he rushed across the tiny space to catch and guide her into a stool at the bar. "Yeah, well, it was... chaotic," he said, trying to give her a worthy excuse. "You were in a rush."

"That's no excuse."

"I've been in touch with Logan off and on all day. You can call him and check me out if you like. Logan made some recommendations and said Axl was an easy kid so... we just hung out here."

"But... why? Why would you do that?"

"Logan said you needed the hours and I had the day off... It's no big deal."

"You could've been *anyone*."

"You thought I was Logan so technically that's not true." He tried not to take offense at her horrified tone but reminded himself she didn't know *him*.

"Yes, but... why would you do this?" she asked again. "How could I not tell you weren't him? *Why* didn't you tell me when I was here earlier?"

A low chuckle left him. "Like I said, it was chaotic. I tried to catch up to you, but you were out of here like a shot. By the time we got to the bottom of the stairs, you were racing out of the parking lot."

She covered her face with her hands and rubbed. "I don't believe this. So why not have Logan call me? Tell me to come back?"

"Logan said it had to be an emergency for you to bring the kid here, and since he wasn't here to care for Axl"—he shrugged—"I thought I'd pitch in for a good cause."

She leaned heavily against the countertop, eyes wide as she processed things.

"I'm the worst mother ever."

"Ah, come on. You're no such thing. You brought your kid to a friend you trusted. Mistaking me for Logan was just a mix-up. You'll laugh about it later, yeah?"

His words drew a weary smile from her lips, and she finally met his gaze, her bright green eyes rueful.

"I just can't believe I did that. I'm so sorry."

He held out his hand and waited until she placed her palm in his. "Let's start over then. I'm Michael Devoncourt, the better-looking, younger twin."

A strangled laugh bubbled out of her and she squeezed his hand.

"Gemma Fiore. Nice to meet you, Michael. Logan mentioned a brother, but I don't remember him saying you were twins."

"Since we're used to it, I guess we don't consider it a big deal. Most people tell us apart by our hair or voice, but since leaving the military, Logan's let his crew cut grow out a bit more."

A laugh left her and he found himself drawn to it. "What?"

"I can only imagine what you thought having someone barge in and throw her child at you."

His chuckle blended with hers until his stomach rumbled loudly. She realized he still held her hand and snatched it away before she jumped to her feet.

"You're hungry. I'll fix you a plate before I take Axl home."

"I'll eat—but only if you join me. You probably haven't had time to eat yourself."

She paused with her hand over a foil-covered take-home box.

"I should probably go. I'm sure you're ready to eat and get out of here."

"Hey, come on. He's fine where he is for now, right?" Michael asked. "After a day of babysitting, the least you can do is keep me company."

He watched as her gaze shifted to her son, and a loving expression flitted over her lips at the sight of Axl's curly head on a pillow, mouth parted as he snoozed.

"You open up that. I'll get plates," he told her, not giving her a chance to leave just yet. He wasn't sure why he wanted her to stay but his curiosity had taken hold. Even though single mothers weren't his thing, he found himself curious to know more about the one in front of him. "So you work at a restaurant?"

"Yes, I'm a chef."

"Does that mean you made all of this?"

"Some," she said, moving back toward the containers.

He set the two plates and utensils down on the counter, aware of the way her head barely came to his shoulder. She smelled of food but in a good way. Grill smoke and something rich and… chocolate? A little coconut that was probably her shampoo. Whatever it was, the combo made him think of good food and drinks by the ocean.

"I'd like to own my own restaurant one day, but until then, it's a pipe dream. And I have other priorities," she said.

His gaze followed hers to where her son slept on the couch, oblivious to their discussion.

"Is it normal for his dad to bail on you?"

She stabbed a bit of filet with a fork and dropped it onto the plate.

"I shouldn't have said that. Not in front of Axl."

"I doubt he understands much about that kind of thing."

Her lips twisted in a wry line.

"He understands when I tell him it's his day with Daddy but then his father doesn't show," she said in a low voice. "I have to stop. Just let the days come and go, and *when* Dennis actually shows up, then we go from there. No expectations."

She plated the food and headed toward the microwave. Michael found himself a bit disconcerted by how well she knew the layout but then reminded himself that all of the apartments were mirror images of each other, with appliances and the like in exactly the same places. Her familiarity wasn't because she spent so much time here—with Logan.

And why would that bother him if she had? "So Logan mentioned you were in the military?"

"Yeah, it was good for me. And I got school paid for, so there's that. What do you do?"

"I'm an architect." He caught the sudden rise of her eyebrows.

"An architect and a doctor. Impressive. Do you have other siblings as driven as you two?"

The wry twist to her lips as she posed the question drew a smile to his own, and once she swapped out the plates, he took the first one to the counter. "No more siblings, but I do have a slew of cousins. Well, kind of. I actually only have two cousins—also twins."

"No way."

He chuckled at her surprise. "Same age, too.

They're both girls. So basically our moms had two apiece and decided four was enough since we were all always underfoot. Plus, the rest of the gang."

"Gang?"

He told her about his pseudo cousins and the Babes.

"Wow. That sounds like the perfect childhood."

Her tone sounded wistful and more than a little sad, and he hated that he'd brought her mood down after finally distracting her from the earlier blunder with his identity and Axl. "It was all right. How about you? Siblings?"

"No. Only child, working mom. Raised mostly by my grandmother."

"Are you close to them now?" It wasn't his business one way or the other but it seemed like the thing to ask.

"My nonna passed before Axl was born but my mom is nearby. She works as a cleaning lady for some rentals on the island. What about you? Any kids?"

He watched as her gaze dropped to his left hand and he had to force himself not to move. "No. Same as Logan."

According to his mother and the Babes, it wasn't normal for men his age to be single. In fact, it wasn't normal for as many of the Babes' children to be single, but quite a few were. Michael chalked it up to watching his parents and the relationships the

Babes had with their spouses. While not perfect—especially in light of his aunt Rayna's recent discovery of his uncle's cheating—the marriages were long-term and seemingly happy. Who wanted to settle for less?

The problem then became finding that person without having to scour the world. Who had time for that working to build a good life? "My career is important to me. I recently had a home built and am putting the finishing touches on. Well, the contractor is, I should say. He's one of us through marriage," he said, referring to Bryson James, Hadley's husband and the secret baby Mary Elizabeth had thought was dead for forty plus years. "Has Logan mentioned the Babes?"

Gemma nodded and carried the second plate over to seat herself beside him.

"He has. I've heard several funny stories about their antics. They sound like modern-day Golden Girls or the Ya Yas."

He chuckled at the descriptions and dug into his food, trying not to inhale it at once due to his hunger and the fact it smelled even better all warmed up. "I suppose in a way they are. Their friendship is something to admire. They're there for each other, no matter what. And they've instilled that same sense of loyalty in all of us."

They tucked into their food for a moment, silence stretching between them.

"This is really great, Gemma. You're a wonderful chef."

"Thanks. It's the least I can do. Logan won't accept payment so I try to pay for his help this way," she said with a laugh.

"Well, that works for me, too."

Axl stirred on the couch and drew his mother's attention, but other than shifting on the cushions, the kid remained sleeping.

"He looks like you, you know," Michael told her. "The dark hair and bright eyes."

"I'm glad. It... makes it easier."

"Things that bad between you and your ex?" Michael felt himself tense on the stool. Surely she'd tell someone if the ex was hurting her or her kid?

"Not bad, just not... anything. He pays child support, which I am totally grateful for, but now that Axl's older and going to daycare, I think he's noticing more. How some of the dads come to pick up their kids. That kind of thing."

"I don't know the guy, but if he isn't meant to be a father, I'd think it would be best if he wasn't around. Things could be worse if he was."

"That's very true. I agree. But that doesn't help Axl have a male influence in his life."

"Are you dating?"

She looked up in surprise but Michael had to choke down his own. He hadn't meant to voice the question aloud. It was one thing to casually chat about the basics of her situation due to the sudden way he'd found himself thrust into her life but quite another to ask something to personal when it meant she might get the wrong idea. "I meant... in the sense of that being helpful for the kid," he scrambled to add.

Gemma held his gaze for a long second or two then blinked and shook her head. "I'm focusing on my child and my career. Nothing else is as important."

He nodded his understanding and let the subject drop before he opened his mouth and said something else he shouldn't.

They finished their food and Gemma passed on the chocolate cake, leaving it for Michael.

"I should get him home and tucked in. Thank you again. I'm so sorry for the mix-up."

"I'll carry him for you."

"Oh, that's not—"

Michael got to the couch first and scooped the boy up without problem. Axl wrapped his chubby arms around him and tucked his face into Michael's neck.

"Ikle."

Gemma's gaze shot from Axl to Michael and he winked at her.

"Like I said, we hit it off. Today was a good day."

11

She really hated bossy men.

On the one hand, Zoey appreciated and understood Logan's concern for her after the incident at the hospital, but on the other?

Male chauvinist—

"You glare at me any harder and your face will freeze like that," Logan said from the chair beside the couch.

"Okay, *Mom*." His deep chuckle sent a shiver through her, because like it or not, it was such a masculine sound and it had been a long time since she'd spent company with a man.

"You want a snack?"

She leaned her still-aching head back on the couch behind her and groaned. "Stop trying to feed me. I've probably gained ten pounds already and we've only been here a day."

"You're beautiful. And I like a little cushion."

Her face flushed in an instant. In all their conversations in the last thirty-plus years, they had never talked about sex. Not in any way. Oh, maybe they'd skirted the edges at times in their letters but only in the sense that she'd broken down a time or two and written about her dating life. One now ex-boyfriend had critiqued her body and hurt her feelings, and she'd poured her heart out in the letter only to regret mailing it afterwards.

Logan's response had been to actually *call her*. She'd let the call go to voicemail, unable to handle whatever she knew he was going to say, and kept the digital recording to this day. When she came down too hard on herself because her just-shy-of-five-feet frame gained weight by looking at food, she made herself play that voicemail.

But now?

Say something. But what? He hadn't said he liked a little cushion *on her*, so why had she taken it that way? His tone? The way he stared at her?

She swallowed hard and took a long sip from her drink. *Do not engage.*

When in doubt, do not engage. It was a mantra she lived by and one she often told her patients and their significant others.

Logan was being unruly, in a subconscious, too-handsome-for-his-own-good kind of way. He didn't realize the impact his words had on people—women, especially.

"So?" he asked. "Do you want something? I think there's some ice cream in the freezer."

"I'm okay. Thanks."

She watched as he shoved himself up from the chair, his long legs eating up the short distance to the kitchen area. She found herself admiring the view and forced her gaze back to the game show they watched. "So, um, how long have you had this cabin?"

"A couple of years. Got it when I was on leave and visiting home. Dad wanted to do some hunting and we didn't have a place to go."

"So you just bought a cabin in the mountains?"

He shut the freezer with a gentle bang and shrugged.

"I like the peacefulness. The beach can get a little hectic, as you know, especially in the summer."

He opened a drawer and pulled out a spoon and then returned to the living area, but instead of going back to the chair, he plopped himself down on the couch beside her so close she tilted sideways and into him before she scrambled to put some distance between them.

"Take a bite."

She'd just resettled the blanket over her legs when he uttered the words and glanced up to find the spoon a breath away from her lips.

"You know you want to."

She glared at him despite the pain that shot through her concussed skull as a result, and he winked at her.

"Might help the headache go away."

"I doubt tha—"

He shoved the spoonful of chocolate ice cream into her mouth and then held the spoon there until she gave in, chuckling because of his antics around the cold deliciousness. "You're mean."

"I beg your pardon. I'm taking care of you like our mothers would want me to."

"If you took me back, I'm sure my mother would do the same."

"Yeah, but see, there you'd be right back at work. Besides, this is more fun."

She swallowed the ice cream and used her fingertips to wipe the excess at the corners of her mouth from the messy delivery. When she glanced over at him, Logan's gaze quickly shifted away, and she blinked at the... weirdness of knowing he'd watched.

"Do you, uh, think you'll be up for a short hike tomorrow?" he asked. "I know you're sore from falling over the stool."

"I doubt my flats will hold up on a hiking trail," she said, reminding him of the fact she hadn't exactly been able to pack or come prepared for a week in the mountains.

"You can go for a while. I can carry you over the rough parts."

"Or," she challenged, "I don't go at all and instead we back to Wilmington."

He shoved the spoon into the container and lifted it to his mouth for a bite and then dug back into it for another spoonful that he held out toward her.

"You gonna argue with me all week about being here?"

He held the spoon steady, waiting on her to accept the bite, but she held his gaze and waited.

Until she found herself distracted by the ice cream melting on the spoon and the fact it would drip on her soon. "Logan."

"Zoey."

"You're being weird."

"Am I?"

Something twisted inside her. Some little something that opened up or let loose, and she realized just how intertwined their lives actually were. He cared for her. For her health and well-being. Why else bring her here and do this? Go to such fuss? "It's going to drip."

"So eat it."

She waited to see if he'd shove the spoon into her mouth again but he didn't move. Even when the melting got worse and the potential drip got bigger. "I only have one set of clothes, Logan. I'd rather they not smell like ice cream. What if it attracts a bear?"

Her heart stopped and chugged to restart when he tilted his head back and laughed, his smile wide and easy and the kind that made women do double takes if they weren't already looking. She should be used to it. She'd seen it before. But she couldn't help but like the fact she'd made him lose his serious doctor face and lighten up.

"I'll protect you from bears, sweetheart."

There it was again. When had he started calling her that? "Lo—"

In the spoon went—just as it dripped. It landed on her chin, and Logan's smile remained when he used his knuckles to wipe it away. "Eat it or wear it, huh?"

"Your choice," he said easily.

She reached out and snagged the container from him and then the spoon. "Get your own then."

THAT EVENING, Logan cleaned up the dinner dishes while Zoey once again dozed on the couch. The fact that she was sleeping so much just proved the extent of her exhaustion.

He smiled at her antics earlier when she'd stolen the ice cream container from him, glad her sense of competitiveness had won out over her worry about her weight. She needed to eat, to be spoiled and pampered, and he intended to make sure that happened this week.

After finishing off the ice cream, she'd gone to the bathroom and washed her face and brushed her teeth with one of the spare toothbrushes he kept on hand for last-minute visits. She probably thought he kept them for overnight guests, but other than Michael and their dad, he'd never brought anyone here.

Kitchen clean, he turned back toward her and leaned his hips against the sink behind him.

He'd given Zoey one of the shirts he kept here for convenience like the toothbrushes. On her short frame, the shirt reached her knees and covered everything a dress would. Maybe more, given the styles.

She'd gone back to the couch and the blanket, and even though he knew she would undoubtedly prefer to sleep there, he couldn't help but think she'd be more comfortable in the bed. She probably figured he would take it given his height, but he wasn't the one injured and recovering.

He crossed the room on silent feet and gently scooped her up in his arms like he had at the hospital to carry her over to the bed. She stirred when he set her down to pull the covers back and tuck her under, and her sleepy gaze held him captive.

"You're sweet even if you are a pain," she said softly, eyes heavy, as though her lids were too much to hold up.

He leaned down and pressed his lips to her forehead, lingering over the kiss. "Right back at you. Sweet dreams, Zo."

He moved away from the bed to give her time to settle in, still debating on the sleeping arrangements. He didn't look forward to a night on a comfortable yet too small couch, but he also didn't want Zoey waking up and braining him with the closest object if he chose to sleep atop the covers next to her. This required pondering.

He quietly let himself out the door and built a small fire in the pit. It was early yet, and despite sleeping most of the day away, Zoey's exhaustion wasn't to be dismissed. She needed this. To recoup and make up for all the sleepless nights she'd suffered due to overwork, stress, and whatever else bothered her.

The low sound of an ATV motor reached his ears, and Logan turned in the direction of his neighbor's home. A single light shone through the trees as Will used the trail between them and made his way to the fire.

He cut the engine the last bit, letting the machine roll slowly until he braked it.

"Everything okay over here?" Will asked. "I thought maybe that was an old-fashioned signal fire."

Logan chuckled and shook his head. "Nah, just passing time."

Will looked at the house with interest.

"Where's your friend?"

Logan followed his gaze to the dimly lit cabin and leaned forward until his elbows rested above his knees. "Asleep. It's going to take her a bit to recover."

"Her, huh?" Will asked, a grin hovering on his lips.

"She's a lifelong friend. Known her since she was born."

"*Oof*. Tough spot to be in."

Will's exclamation seemingly held all of the frustration and indecisiveness Logan felt. "Exactly. You want a drink?"

"I'm good, thanks. Just wanted to check on things. Groceries okay? Need anything else? I'm heading there tomorrow to get something fixed. I can stop again if need be."

"Thanks. I'll text you and let you know, but nothing comes to mind at the moment. You doing okay?"

Will stared into the fire, and Logan couldn't help but think the man was hanging around for a reason. Logan settled himself back in the Adirondack chair and gave the man time to speak—or not speak—as he liked.

Finally Will inhaled and let out a rough exhale.

"Just... wondering if it was worth it."

"If what was?"

Will stared into the fire for a long moment. "I lost a buddy today. He's one of the twenty-two," Will said, referencing the number of veterans who commit suicide in a single day.

"Ah, man, I'm sorry to hear that."

Will's expression became distant, focused on whatever he remembered.

"I lost a lot of buddies over there. And after all that, we just up and leave it behind? The equipment? The guns?"

Logan had heard the news report as well. Millions and millions of American dollars had been left behind for the enemy to use. Against the US and their other enemies. It wasn't right. And he knew there wasn't a single soldier, them included, that didn't feel one way or another about it and need a safe place to talk. "Some things don't make sense."

"You can say that again."

"Guess this is where we have to wait and see what happens and be prepared for when it does." Logan watched as Will's hands tightened over the bars of the ATV in response to his statement. "What'd you do over there?"

Logan couldn't help but think it was harder for those who'd seen battle than those in relative safety on the bases and hospitals. The most danger he'd faced was when he traveled into and out of the base.

"Little bit of everything."

Logan narrowed his gaze, understanding the lack of answer as his answer. Will seemed friendly enough, but he also carried a vibe that made it clear he wasn't a man to be messed with.

"I'd better get home," Will said, twisting the key to start the ATV. "Let me know if you need anything."

"Come back tomorrow evening for dinner. Steaks," Logan said. "I'll introduce you to Zoey. Say, six?"

Will hesitated for a moment but then nodded. "Yeah. I'll bring something."

"You don't have to."

The ATV's engine roaring up and Will putting it into gear drowned out Logan's words. He shut up and sat back in the chair once again, lifting a hand in goodbye as Will turned the four-wheeler away and headed back toward the woods separating their property.

Logan wasn't sure why he'd invited the man over, because he'd rather keep Zoey to himself, but he also knew Zoey's presence had a soothing effect on people. Maybe that would be the case with Will. It wouldn't be a counseling session or work but friends being friendly. Sometimes that was all people needed. Zoey included.

Even if he wanted to be more.

The following afternoon, Michael stood in front of the makeshift desk and stared down at the house plans he'd worked so hard on. It was perfect. Absolutely perfect.

So what was missing?

No matter how many hours he pored over the plans, he couldn't shake the feeling that something just wasn't right.

"Did you figure it out?" Bryson James asked as he entered the room.

Michael turned and watched as his cousin's contractor husband came in with a grin on his face. Considering the happy couple were still in the honeymoon phase, Michael supposed it was a good thing. "No."

"But you're sure something's off with the plans?"

Michael straightened from where he'd braced

himself over the desk and nodded. "I just can't put my finger on it."

"Kinda hard to make changes at this stage, but I'll give it a shot if you ever figure it out," the man said.

"Yeah, thanks. Hopefully it'll come to me soon."

"You want to hang out? Hadley's cooking sides and I plan to grill. We've got plenty if you're hungry."

Home-cooked meals were hard to come by as a bachelor, at least edible ones, and while he appreciated the offer, he shook his head, thinking of a certain brunette and her little boy. "Thanks, though. I'm gonna head downtown for dinner. Hit a couple places."

He blamed his thoughts of a certain brunette on his lack of female companionship of late. Maybe going downtown, having a drink, and listening to music...

After carrying Axl to bed, he'd found himself reluctant to leave Gemma's company despite how exhausted she looked. He'd wanted to linger. Help in some way.

Everything about her was wrong. The baggage of her child, the drama in her life with her ex. Her working two jobs to make ends meet—which he didn't understand her having to do if her ex paid child support. Surely she used that money to help keep a roof over Axl's head? To help feed him? He'd wanted to ask about the reason for two jobs but knew it wasn't any of his business. It was just another example of how, from start to finish, she was everything he didn't want in a woman. In a companion.

So why had he spent the entire day thinking about her?

That will end tonight.

"You sure you're all right?" Bryson asked. "You seem a little distracted."

Michael ran a hand through his hair and left the plans that stayed at the house during the build. "Nah, just ready for the weekend," he said. "See you Monday if not before, yeah?"

"Yeah. Have fun."

Michael left Bryson behind and exited the house, letting the other man lock up.

He got in his Jeep and drove slowly down the street by the boardwalk. There were people everywhere, walking, riding bikes, carrying beach chairs as they made their way toward the ocean. He took care to watch for them, turning up the radio and cruising along with the top back and doors off.

Today was one of those unbelievably perfect summer days. The kind that made him take a breath of the salt air and ocean breeze and just be glad to be alive because everything looked right with the world. At least this part of the world right now.

Shoving the problematic house plans aside, he kept going and enjoyed the drive. Traffic wasn't too bad heading toward the northern end of the island, where he had a small condo, but he knew in another hour or so it would be bumper to bumper. He needed to get showered and changed in ten minutes flat to beat the rush off the island as beachgoers started leaving for dinner.

He showered and was back in his Jeep Wrangler in eight minutes. That was another thing about living on the coast. Dressing up was for special occasions only, and summer wear meant pulling on clean shorts, comfortable shoes, and a T-shirt.

He headed north toward Wilmington, deciding to try a place he'd heard Bryson raving about as having great food. In a town teeming with restaurants and bistros, bars, and the like, he'd found himself in a rut going to the same places. Maybe the change of pace would shake things up. He could find a seat at the bar, get a good meal. Make an effort to meet someone who wasn't a single mom.

This trip took longer due to the traffic off of the island, and the sun had sunk deeper into the sky by the time he arrived. He made his way inside and noted the wait for a table, but the bar area had open seating.

As he made his way to it, he realized the bar also had a good view of the kitchen behind a glass wall, and he found himself staring at a particular brunette who caught his eye.

Was it Gemma? She'd never told him where she

worked, so if it was her, he hoped she didn't consider his appearance stalking.

As though sensing his perusal, the woman turned and locked gazes with him. An invisible fist slugged him in the stomach when Gemma's gaze narrowed as though she was having those exact thoughts.

Giving her a rueful smile, he shrugged and took one of the empty stools.

"What'll you have?" the bartender asked.

He placed his order for a local brew and watched as Gemma went back to doing whatever she was doing behind the glass. It made him wonder where Axl was this evening, but then he reminded himself it wasn't any of his business.

The bartender brought his drink and took his food order, and Michael grinned when he ordered the chef's special with an additional comment for the chef to surprise him.

The bartender gave Michael an odd look but carried the order to the back. Michael waited, sipping his frosted mug and watching as Gemma went through the latest food orders to come in. Other than a quick glance over her shoulder toward him, she didn't respond.

In the corner, a guy set up to start playing guitar, and more people crowded into the restaurant as the evening progressed. He was focused on the musician when a plate landed in front of him, a slender hand withdrawing before he could snag it.

"What are you doing here?"

He lifted his eyebrows in surprise. "Is that any way to greet a customer?"

"It is when it's suspicious," she said under her breath.

"Nothing suspicious about it," he told her, smiling. "Hadley and Bryson—my cousins—had dinner here recently, and Bryson was raving about the place. I thought I would give it a shot. You," he said, lifting a finger from the mug he held, "were an unexpected surprise."

"Really?" Her head cocked to one side.

"Really."

"Chef!"

"Be right there," she told the bartender, who was on his way back with orders once again.

He nodded his understanding to pass on the news and disappeared.

"Well, if that's the case, enjoy. You said to surprise you so... it's not on the menu. Owner refuses. But I wanted to say thanks again for babysitting. I still can't believe I didn't realize you weren't Logan."

He chuckled at the memory, knowing it would always bring a smile to his lips. "It's all good. Believe it or not, I had fun. He's a cute kid."

A man overdressed in a suit kept shifting his

attention from the blond he flirted with at the other end of the U-shaped bar. After a moment, the man headed toward them from behind the bar where Gemma stood. Tension flooded Gemma when she tracked Michael's gaze.

"Gemma, we have waitstaff to take orders. You should be in the back," the man all but growled.

His gaze had shifted from Gemma to Michael, and Michael gave as good as he got in regard to the glare. "And here I was just about to post a review about the wonderful customer service," Michael said.

That made the man glower even darker, and Michael felt as though he faced a schoolyard bully as the man sized him up. Overall, Michael wasn't impressed. Oh, the guy obviously had looks and money, given the cut of the suit and the Rolex on his arm, but other than a pretty face, he didn't seem to have much substance.

So who was the guy to her? "Michael Devoncourt," he said, holding a hand out toward the man.

"Dennis Keeton, owner of the Blue Palm."

Gemma all but rolled her eyes at the man's bragging but didn't speak. His gut told him the situation wasn't on the level.

"How do you know my Gemma?" the man asked, placing his palms on Gemma's shoulders.

Michael lifted a hand and covered his smile as

Gemma huffed and pointedly shrugged the hands off of her.

Michael watched as Dennis's face took on a ruddy hue, but he managed to keep his pretty-boy smile in place despite the obvious tension and shutdown.

"I should get back to work," Gemma said, her gaze shifting between them nervously.

"I'll see you afterwards," Michael said, daring her to argue given the way Dennis was acting. "Just like last night."

Oh, yeah. Dennis of the Blue Palm was possessive, all right. Despite the wedding ring on his finger. The man's expression tightened with fury. If Gemma hadn't shrugged off the man's hold so quickly, Michael would've thought more of it, but now? The guy wasn't fooling anyone.

"I... um, yeah, I look forward to it. I'll finish up in another hour."

"I'll be right here."

The flaring of his nostrils and darkening of his expression revealed Dennis's thoughts on the matter. Not that Michael cared. And until he could get Gemma alone to set the record straight as to their connection, he wasn't going to assume anything. Just because the man wanted her didn't mean the feeling was mutual.

"What is this about last night? You were scheduled to work last night," Dennis said.

"I did work," she said to Dennis.

"Is there a problem?" Michael asked.

"Yes, I'm afraid there is. My chef has momentarily gone rogue," the guy said, glaring at the plate in front of Logan. "That is not a current item on the menu, and as such, it would be unfair of us to allow you to enjoy it while denying our other guests. Allow me to get you something—"

Michael's hands shot out and gripped the plate, making nothing short of a tug-of-war necessary to get it away from him. "This isn't going anywhere but in my stomach."

"Then you should eat before it gets cold," Gemma said in a rush, glancing around them.

Michael was aware they'd gained the attention of those nearby but he didn't care. The plate Gemma had fixed for him wasn't going anywhere, and if Dennis thought otherwise, Michael was prepared to set him straight.

"Let's let him eat, shall we? Enjoy."

"I'll be in the kitchen to speak to you soon," Dennis said.

Gemma released a rolled-eyed exhale and dipped her head in Michael's direction, obviously not wanting to leave the two of them alone. She spun on her heel and quickly made her way back to the kitchen. Michael watched her go, making no bones about enjoying the view.

Once she was behind the glass and counter,

Michael turned his attention back on Dennis and smirked at the man's steady glare.

"I don't know who you are, but stay away from her."

"And why would I do that?" Michael asked, even though he'd been telling himself to do the same thing earlier. "She's single." He pointedly glanced down at the man's hand. "And you're not. Does your wife know you have a thing for one of your employees?"

Michael held the man's furious gaze for a long moment until the guy finally pasted on a fake smile and told him to *have a nice evening.*

Michael knew exactly what the man wished for him and silently returned the sentiment. After good ol' Dennis stalked away, Michael picked up his fork and dug into the rapidly cooling meal.

He wasn't sure what it was called but it made for a beautiful plate. Pasta and shrimp, sun-dried tomatoes, hints of other seafood, some bits of something he couldn't identify but that tasted divine, all in a buttery wine sauce that made his mouth water.

"Chef suggested you try this with your meal, sir. On the house," the bartender said, setting a glass of wine in front of him. A folded napkin accompanied the glass, and Michael unfolded it once the bartender walked away.

Sorry about that. –G

She had nothing to be sorry for. As to the wine...

he wasn't much of a wine drinker, but he murmured his thanks and took a sip after another bite. The burst of flavor brought out the richness of the meal and made it taste even better if that was possible.

It was amazing. More than amazing—it was so good he didn't have a word for it. He could taste the salt and tanginess, cream and garlic, and so much more. It was art—in the form of food. He'd had some good cooking in his life, but he didn't ever remember anything as tasty as this.

He tucked into the deliciousness with gusto but followed Dennis's movements as he made his way behind the glass wall and stood over Gemma's shoulder as she cooked. Gemma kept her cool and simply ignored the man yammering on, but when she glanced up and found Michael's eyes on her once more, she seemed embarrassed and looked away.

Michael knew a power play when he saw it. Dennis postured and waved his hands as he talked, putting on a show for anyone back there to listen in on. Embarrassing her in front of her staff.

Michael didn't want to upset her, but if the guy was giving her a hard time, he was more than willing to step in on her behalf.

Why?

Because Axl didn't deserve to have his mama harassed. Michael didn't know the full story but Gemma's body language told him a lot. Maybe at one time she and Dennis had shared something, but it was over between them now—because Gemma said so, not because of Dennis.

Gemma's food was beyond compare, and as the owner, the man should be on his knees thanking her for continuing to work for him, not giving her a hard time.

Michael sipped the wine and continued to stare as Gemma said something to her employer. The jerk stiffened up like a board, his neck turning as red as the silk handkerchief tucked into his tailored pocket.

The man looked to be about to grab her arm when Gemma sidestepped and held up the forked utensil she'd been using, brandishing it with a warning glare and a comment of her own. Michael stiffened, ready to stand and jump over the bar to get to her, when Dennis backed away with a glance around and a final comment.

Gemma watched him go before her gaze shifted to Michael's and he gave her a wink and a nod of approval.

13

L ogan had doused the fire and come inside the cabin when he heard Zoey cry out in her sleep.

He hustled toward the bed, bending over her tiny figure under the blanket. "Zo?"

Her eyes were closed, face squeezed up in a pinched expression as she tossed her head on the pillow.

"No. *Noooo!*"

"Hey, hey, hey, you're okay."

She sat upright so fast he didn't have time to get out of the way, and her head hit the bone of his shoulder. He quickly grabbed her to hold her, kissing the top of her head and cuddling her close. "Zoey? Zoey, baby, it's just a dream. You're having a bad dream. Shh."

Her nails dug into his skin, eliciting a wince, but

the pain didn't last. As quickly as she'd grasped hold, she let go, smoothing her fingers over the crescent moons left behind.

"I'm sorry. I hurt you."

"It's fine. You're fine. Come here."

He tugged her closer until she was up and over his lap. Maybe he was playing with fire where his feelings and emotions were concerned regarding her, but right now he didn't care. She needed comfort and he planned to give it.

He scooted them both until his back rested against the headboard of the bed, cuddling her until her breathing calmed and the smattering of tears produced by her dream and leaking from her eyes dried up.

He thumbed the remaining tears off her cheek, and she snuggled her forehead into his neck. "You want to talk about it?"

She swallowed audibly and seconds passed while he waited.

"It was just... what happened at the hospital. But then it changed."

"Changed how?" he asked, hoping that talking about it would help her process things in such a way the nightmares would go away.

"You came into the room and... he hurt you. There was so much blood."

He tightened his arms around her and squeezed her, the thought of her dreams being of *him* sending a pang of desire and protection straight to his heart. "I'm right here, baby. You're the one who got hurt."

"I know but... it's just how it played out, you know? Dreams are weird."

Dreams were indeed weird. Whether dreams of actual events or fearsome possibilities.

They sat there in silence for a few minutes, and he waited for her to protest her position on his lap and the endearments that kept slipping from his lips. But when seconds ticked on and she didn't, he loosened his hold a little and let himself enjoy the moment.

Zoey yawned. Then yawned again. Squirmed a bit and curled the arm closest to him around his back and side, her injured arm already secured to her chest by the sling.

Barely daring to breathe, he glanced down to see her lashes getting heavy.

He should put her down. Get her comfortable in the bed. Instead he held her long after she fell asleep, more comfortable and relaxed than he'd been in a very long time.

Maybe just this once... she wouldn't mind if he kept holding her.

MICHAEL WAITED at the bar for Gemma's shift to end, opening a tab and enjoying the music and activity of a busy night on the town. He didn't go out much, not like in his younger years, so this was a treat in multiple ways.

He spent most nights working on the high-rise buildings he specialized in, but his pet projects were the residential plans he'd been creating more of late for friends and family.

In the last year, he'd designed several homes, including Isabel and Everett's new beach house. It was the most expansive single-family home he'd designed to date. But with the billionaire's budget and free rein to add features that the large family of Babes and extended cousins could use, Michael had been able to go all out. Indoor pool, sauna, lazy river to an outdoor pool. Game room, theater room, fire pit, outside kitchen, an office for Everett, and a large art studio for Isabel, along with the regular household rooms like a kitchen, dining, and multiple bedrooms for their future family.

Maybe that was why he was so stuck with his own home design? Had he incorporated so much of himself into their dream home that he struggled to make his own meaningful? Design wise, the two didn't compare, but he'd put a lot of time and effort into creating a space he loved.

He still pondered the question when Gemma reappeared. The chef's smock was gone, and now she wore a snug Bon Jovi T-shirt and black leggings that hugged her curvy frame to perfection. "Do you need to rush home to Axl or can you stay for a dance?"

She seemed taken aback by the question, and he watched as her expressions ranged from surprise to contemplation to being flustered.

"Um, he's with my mom so... I have some time."

He took her hand and led her toward the dance floor in front of the lone singer. The guy knew his ballads, and there were four other couples on the floor swaying in time to the music.

Gemma seemed a bit self-conscious so he stepped closer and tugged her into his arms. Her head came to his chin, and he found himself lightly brushing it against her temple to feel her soft skin.

Then had to remind himself she wasn't his type.

They swayed back and forth from one song to another until Gemma stiffened in his hold, and he drew back to look at her, following her stare to the corner of the room where her boss glared at them. Michael turned his attention back to her and asked, "Do you want to go somewhere else?"

She shook her head.

"No. I'm not on the clock. There's no rule that says I can't dance but... I really should head home."

"One more then." He smiled at her and tugged her against him, closer than ever. Over her head, Michael met her ex's gaze and the man's anger was tangible. He turned on his heel and stalked out of sight. "Tell me about your boss."

"What do you want to know?"

"He's very possessive of you."

"That's a word for it," she muttered.

"What's your word for it?"

"Controlling ex?"

Surprise shot through him even though he'd figured it was something along those lines. "He's married." And she didn't seem like the type. But then what did he know about her?

"He is married... now." She inhaled deeply and sighed. "Dennis and I have known each other awhile. We worked at the same restaurant and dated off and on. Then he got a manager job here and asked me to come, too. I hired on as a chef, got pregnant, and found out he'd been dating the owner's daughter all along. Her father offered him the Blue Palm as a wedding present and the rest is history."

"Sounds like the woman's father really wanted her off of his hands. You know you're better off without him."

"I am well aware."

"So why are you still working here?"

A second or two passed before she answered. "It pays okay. And the few times I've seen better jobs and applied, I wasn't hired."

"Do you think he's keeping you from getting hired elsewhere?"

"I wouldn't be surprised. But he's my main reference as manager and owner..."

"You're letting him control you."

"I'm keeping a roof over my child's head and paying my bills," she said, stopping to stand and stare up at him. "I won't apologize for that."

"You don't need to apologize for anything but surely you see—"

"Good night, Michael."

She turned away and left him standing on the dance floor. After a moment's hesitation, he followed her toward the exit and caught up with her in the parking lot. "Hey. Gemma, come on. Wait a second."

"I need to get home," she said, opening the door to her car.

"Gemma, *wait*. I wasn't being critical," Michael said. The wry twist to her mouth and expression let him know what she thought of his lie. "Okay, fine, so maybe I was being a little critical. But not in a mean way."

"There's another way?" She climbed into her vehicle.

He held the car door open. "Yeah, there is. I'm concerned, that's all. You seem like a nice woman and Axl is a great kid. I'd hate to see some jerk taking advantage of you."

Her shoulders lowered a bit as she accepted his words and she lifted a hand to twist the keys to start the vehicle.

"Thanks. But I don't need your concern. I can take care of myself."

"If he's keeping you from getting another job…"

"What? Are you going to play hero for me? How? And in exchange for what? I can take care of myself."

"I don't doubt that. But that doesn't mean you can't accept a helping hand every now and again— for your son's sake if nothing else."

Her hands fisted over the wheel so tightly her knuckles turned white in the darkened interior. The breeze blew her hair into her face, and since he held her door and she couldn't close it, he liked the way it floated across her cheek before she tucked it behind her ear.

"Why? It's a simple question," she said, her gaze narrowing even more when he didn't immediately speak.

"Can't a person just help someone?"

"In my experience, there are always catches."

Yeah, she was right about that. Everything had a condition to it, but since he wasn't even sure where this conversation was leading or why he'd followed her to her car, he scrambled for an answer she'd be happy with. "I wouldn't mind more of your cooking."

His response brought a soft huff from her chest before she shook her head and shoved the car into Drive.

"Close the door."

"Gemma, come on. Talk to me."

"Good night, Michael."

He knew what she'd expected him to say. What

she *expected* from men in general considering her ex had pulled the rug out from under her to marry someone else due to what the woman offered. There were far too many people in the world who would lie, cheat, and steal in order to get a leg up and with no regard for the others in their life and the impact it might have on them.

Michael shut the door and watched her drive away, shaking his head at her lead foot and the way she rolled over a speed bump like it wasn't even there.

Other than possibly her driving being an issue, he found her attractive, intelligent. Witty. Not to mention a fantastic cook.

Could he handle more of her? Sure. But then Axl's face appeared in his mind's eye, and Michael couldn't help but think he'd prefer the single 'her,' not necessarily the motherly one responsible for a kid and pull-ups and the chaos that came with being a single parent. One day, sure. But getting an insta-kid was definitely putting the cart in front of the horse.

"Beautiful women are rarely worth the trouble," said a voice out of the dark.

Michael turned to find Dennis hugging the shadows of the parking lot like the creep he proved to be. He didn't respond to Dennis's comment and instead put his feet in motion toward his Jeep.

"Stay away from her."

Michael turned to face the man, grinning in such a way that threw out a challenge. "Not gonna happen, man. She's free to see who she wants—and from what she told me, you only have yourself to blame for that."

14

I will not meet your friend wearing your oversized T-shirt and gym shorts," Zoey said. "Or a scrub set from the hospital that has blood stains on it still."

Logan leaned against the counter and watched as Zoey paced the floor of the living room the following morning, her hair sticking up in the back from where she'd slept on it. "You could just wear the T-shirt. Make it a dress."

Her low growl left him grinning from ear to ear. "Will isn't going to give a care what you wear, sweetheart. I think he could just use some company right now."

Logan hadn't meant to speak of the man's issues, especially considering Zoey was supposed to be resting. But at his words, Zoey's pacing stopped and she turned to face him, so he figured he'd use her desire to help others to accomplish his goal.

"What do you mean?"

Logan swiped a hand over his face. "He lost a buddy yesterday. A vet to suicide. I thought inviting him over might help get his mind on other things. And since you're wanting so badly to get back to work..."

"So *now* I'm allowed to work?"

"This is an exception," he said.

"Uh-huh. Does he know I'm a counselor?" she asked.

"No. I didn't mention that."

"Because he wouldn't talk to me if he knew?"

"Because it didn't come up and... I don't know. When I called him to pick up the groceries that night, I told him you work at the hospital, but I don't believe I ever said in what capacity."

"Well, either way, that still doesn't change the fact I have no clothes."

"I'm not taking you to town. I won't risk you jumping in someone's car and speeding away like you did that night Shelly Rogers kissed your jerk of a boyfriend."

"How could I not be upset? We were going together! At least we were *supposed* to be. Who knows what might've happened if Shelly had kept her long legs out of the picture. Wyatt and I might've been married by now."

"If you and Wyatt were still together, it would be him, you, and a side chick or three. Come on, Zo. Get real."

She glowered at him and he glowered right back. Why were they fighting again? "Look, take a gander in the closet. See what you find to make you feel more comfortable. I know I have some jeans in there somewhere. Shorts, too. Would wearing one of them make you feel better?"

"What would really make me feel better is if I had my own clothes—which I can get *at home*."

"Well, since we aren't there, I suppose you'll have to make do."

Her mutinous expression left him gritting his teeth in a struggle not to smile. "You're not going to win this one, sweetheart. Give it up."

"What are you going to do when I tell this neighbor you've kidnapped me?"

He moved closer until he stood toe-to-toe and stared down at her. "I guess if I think that's going to happen, I'll have to figure out a way to shut you up." He lowered his head until his nose almost touched hers and he saw her eyes widen. "How do you think I'll do it?"

She swallowed and blinked at him.

"Do what?"

He let his grin widen and watched how her face flushed. Maybe he wasn't the only one feeling the heat? Could it be?

The mental debate of whether to shoot his shot and let her know in no uncertain terms how he felt about her surged through him, tempered only by the fear of crashing and burning. Once said, the words —the actions—couldn't be taken back. But it risked everything. Their lifelong friendship. The ease they had within the group of "cousins." The future and what could play out.

Things could go wrong. Relationships fell apart all the time.

But some... didn't.

He lifted his hand and stroked a tendril of hair away from her cheek, tucking it carefully behind her ear. Once finished, he allowed his thumb to stroke the freckled velvet of her cheek.

His mind scrambled with what-ifs and some ideas that should make him blush, but the urge to gamble and fight to win no matter the fallout surged strong and sure within him.

He heard the breath she inhaled, felt the way it shuddered into her lungs. Saw the way she parted her lips to draw more in as though unable to catch her breath.

Did he dare?

He lightly touched her lower lip with his thumb, brushing it gently back and forth.

"Logan..."

She took a stumbling step back and then

another, an awkward huff of a laugh erupting from her as she crossed the floor to the fridge.

"You know, they say revenge is sweet. I'll h-have to think of some way to get you back for bringing me here."

He pondered her words a long moment. "Do you want to kidnap me, Zo?"

"I want you to stop messing with me," she said with a slam of the door. She waved a hand in the air toward him as though swatting at a fly. "*That*... That's not funny."

"I wasn't trying to be."

"So, what, now you're pretending to flirt with me just to get me to cooperate? Does that work with the women you know?"

"Do you think that's why I'm flirting with you?"

Face flaming with red-hot color, she stalked down the hall toward the only other room and entered the bathroom, slamming the door behind her.

"You can't escape, Zoey. You have nowhere to go."

"But... you're being ridiculous! We have a pact!"

He grinned as he made his way to the door and leaned against the wooden molding. "That was only because of Devon and Oz and it's over now anyway. They're together or have you forgotten?"

"Logan, I mean it, stop messing with me," she yelled through the door. "It's weird!"

"Sweetheart, trust me, you'll know when I mess with you. Besides, what if you liked it?"

A defiant shriek of frustration from within the bathroom was her response.

His thoughts returned to that moment, that *second*, when she'd stared up at him and her gaze had revealed her thoughts. He had enough experience to know when a woman noticed him—or was at least intrigued by him—and despite the fact Zoey didn't want to think of him that way because of the pact they'd made while watching Devon and Oz navigate a disastrously painful breakup, she did.

And that?

That was a start he planned to take full advantage of now that he'd crossed the bridge and lit the fire to burn it behind him.

15

Zoey avoided Logan the best she could all day, even though she felt childish in the doing. If he entered the cabin, she left. If he followed her to the porch, she walked to the hammock. It didn't matter that her body screamed in complaint due to the ongoing soreness. She reminded herself that the more she moved, the better and faster the soreness would dissipate and her body would return to normal.

Logan finally seemed to get the hint and left her alone other than a few barked words to come eat lunch.

She fell asleep in the hammock, and when she woke up, she stared at the sun filtering through the canopy of trees above her head, no closer to discerning his strange behavior than she had been when it had happened.

Had he meant what he said? The way he'd acted? Or was he so used to flirting with women that he'd just done it automatically?

They were friends. Just friends. Why, after thirty-two years of existence, would Logan suddenly notice her as anything else?

It didn't make sense.

That evening, she lingered in the shower until the water turned cold and got out to dress. When she'd entered the cabin, she'd discovered Logan had left clothing on the couch for her, and even though he was nowhere to be found, she considered the gesture sweet.

Stop it. He's not sweet he's... he's...

Unable to settle on an adjective, Zoey yanked on the clothes and did her best to make them fit. She fidgeted with the stitched hem of Logan's shirt until it rested in a neat yet sloppy style and glared at the copious amount of denim rolled up on her legs just so her feet were exposed. Logan's legs were ridiculously long, and despite all her efforts, she felt like little kid playing dress-up.

She'd styled the T-shirt so that it hung off of one shoulder since she'd given up the battle of moving it back into place every couple of seconds and managed to make the outfit look as best as it possibly could under the circumstances. Thankfully the bra she'd worn to work the day of the incident was the transitional kind with straps that fastened a variety of ways, so she didn't have a visible strap on her shoulder.

Welcome back to the eighties, she mused as she stared at herself in the mirror.

With the T-shirt front tucked and the sides and back hanging, it could've actually been cute if not for the mega-cuffed pant legs. Or the fact her only shoes were dress flats. Those skewed the entire look.

A knock sounded at the bathroom door, and after a deep breath, she reluctantly opened it. As a counselor, she couldn't exactly continue playing the avoidance game. Not and be honest when it came to making suggestions to her clients.

"You look great."

She met Logan's gaze in the mirror in front of her and glared. He grinned back at her, his gaze warming the longer he stared.

One of these days, she mused. One of these days, she would—

"Come on, sweetheart. I think I hear Will heading this way."

Sweetheart. Baby. Honey. Over the span of the day, the list of endearments and names Logan used to refer to her continued to grow despite her behavior toward him. It was weird.

And that comment about *trust me, you'll know when I mess with you?*

What did that *mean* exactly?

That he *wasn't?*

If that was the case, what was with all of the winks and smiles and comments? Simple conversation that somehow seemed flirtatious?

She watched him go, her thoughts keeping her feet pinned to the floor. Because it sure felt like something had shifted between them. Something big that made all the secret, silent, prickly parts of her wonder if those things could mean more. Logan had never acted that way toward her. Friendly, yes. Protective, sure. But flirty?

The pact they'd made so many years ago, though... One of Rayna's twin daughters, Devon, and Logan's best friend, Oz, had dated, gotten engaged, and then broken up.

To say the fallout was painful put it mildly. Oz had been devastated when Devon left Carolina Cove. They all had, because they'd watched the two grow from puppy-eyed teenagers to college sweethearts who really seemed like the perfect pair.

Until they weren't.

The "cousins" and friends had wound up choosing sides even though their hearts broke for both of them. Some said Devon was right to chase her dreams and end things so they didn't wind up divorced. Others said Oz was right to not quit his steady job and chase Devon to New York City when she'd taken an unpaid internship that might not pan out.

But witnessing Oz's recovery from being jilted

and left behind just before the walk to the altar had left scars on all of them.

Add to that her own experiences with so-called men and those of her mother's wherein she'd divorced her first husband and been widowed twice over since, the Babes, *as well as* her patients, and it made it really hard to believe in love. Because it always, always ended in pain.

Why would anyone want to take the risk? How could it possibly be worth it?

She was surrounded by people who in one way or another had been utterly decimated by love. Because those who meant the most were the ones to hurt you the worst.

Recovering from a breakup, being willing to brave trying again... was nothing short of a miracle, in her estimation.

Life was a risk but love was... more. It was dangerous and murky, and it didn't hold back when it came to causing the pain she witnessed—felt—on a daily basis.

She forced her thoughts away by running cold water over her inner wrists as a distraction.

Logan had left the cabin after his comment about hearing Will's arrival, and her mind shifted to thoughts of the man she was about to meet. Logan and his kidnapping aside, she reminded herself of her life's mission.

She wanted to help people. Help them through

dark times and good and all of the chaos in between. She considered it her calling from a higher power.

But right now? Why did she feel so tired? Was it the incident at work? Or was Logan right? Was she burning out?

Why else would she question her abilities and dedication to a job she loved?

The difference between how she'd felt starting out years ago and now...

"Zo!"

She turned off the water and dried her hands, glared in the mirror one last time, and adjusted the strap of her sling to help hold the material in place off of her shoulder.

She certainly didn't want to accidentally flash anyone due to the oversized shirt—especially Logan. Because that would be weird. Right?

She left the bathroom and made her way through the house and out the cabin doors. A man stood talking with Logan beside the fire, his broad shoulders bigger and wider than Logan's, which were nothing to laugh at.

The man also stood a good three inches taller than Logan, which put him at about six feet five inches, and once she moved closer, she found herself craning her neck to meet his gaze. "Hi."

Logan introduced her to Will, and the man's gaze crinkled at the corners as he towered over her and extended his monstrous hand.

Seriously. She looked like a toddler next to him and barely reached his elbow in the process of shaking his hand. "It's nice to meet you, Will."

"You, too." Will shifted his gaze to the sling on her arm. "Are you feeling better? Logan mentioned an incident at the hospital."

"Yeah, I am. I'm just sore at this stage. I get to remove the sling tomorrow, though."

"Will, you want a drink?"

Logan held out a bottle, and the man's massive paw stretched out to take it, swallowing it whole like he had her hand.

In short order, they got the food situation started inside the cabin at the counter and then returned outside to sit and stare into the flames as the sky darkened and the mountaintop came alive with the sights and sounds of summer in the woods.

She had to admit it was beautiful. Fireflies blinked randomly, the stars overhead shone brightly, and the sound of a nearby creek made for peaceful background noise.

They ate mostly in silence, with the guys sharing a few comments on the food.

Zoey glanced at Logan and held his gaze for a moment. If he wanted her to try to talk to his friend, he needed to give her space to do so.

Logan narrowed his gaze as if in warning to behave herself as far as asking for an escape mission off the mountain before he got up with the excuse of getting more firewood.

"So do you live on the mountain year-round?" she asked.

"Yeah. My family's been here a long time. Came over in the late 1700s."

"Oh, wow."

"Yeah, my ancestors were some of the first. After I got out of the military, it just made sense to come back and stay."

"How long did you serve?"

"Twenty-four years."

"That's dedication. You and Logan are to be commended for your service."

"It was a living. One I was good at. What about you? What do you do?"

Oh, that took a moment to answer. "Hmm. I'm actually a counselor."

A rough laugh emerged from Will's chest.

"What? Is that funny?"

"Nah. I suppose that's why you seem easy to talk to. And why Logan was so insistent I come over tonight."

She grinned and shrugged. "In all honesty, it was probably more for my benefit than yours. I'm a bit of a workaholic, and being here has me climbing the walls and driving Logan insane."

She caught the look the man gave Logan, who stood in the distance stacking chopped wood in his arms. "He only wanted to help, you know. So do I. It's kind of in our nature as doctors."

"I suppose you're right," the man murmured. "Thanks, but I'm fine."

"Are you?"

He stared her down and she held his gaze until she got another awkward grin.

"I bet you're good at your job."

"I try to be. Look, Will, Logan mentioned you lost a friend recently. I'm sorry for your loss. Were you close friends?"

"No. Not really. But he was the second man we've lost that way in less than a year."

That's all the information Will offered, and she waited patiently, hoping he would share more.

One of the biggest mistakes people made when talking to friends was that they didn't stay quiet and *listen* to the other person talk. Sometimes silence was the best motivator to let them continue as their thoughts allowed.

After a moment, he said, "Charlie was a good guy. We got out about the same time, but when he got back to the States, he found his wife with his best friend and their house foreclosed on. Add in PTSD and I guess he just couldn't deal."

"One of those things would be enough to devastate someone. All three? He needed help."

"Yeah. He did."

"It doesn't make life any easier, though. Especially when someone you care about hurts themselves."

"Definitely not."

"It's also hard to take that advice when emotions run so high. Especially regarding love. To be honest, it's the biggest issue my patients have. Dealing with the pain and heartbreak and fallout. Trying to rebuild themselves afterwards."

Will took a long pull from his drink and stared into the flames.

"You do know there's nothing you could have done to save him, right? Charlie made the decision to take his own life. Maybe if you'd been aware and reached out, it might have postponed things, but it wouldn't have changed the outcome. Not if that was Charlie's intention."

A long silence followed her words but eventually Will nodded. "Yeah, I know. It just hit close to home and there's just too many dying. Vets, I mean. People don't get it."

"Get what?" she asked softly.

"We go and serve and we're glad to do it, but when we get back... it's hard to fit in again. You've missed birthdays, family events. Holidays. Moments that become private jokes that you weren't a part of. From then on, you're always an outsider because of it. People have memories you don't have and you can't get those back."

Will leaned back from where he'd moved,

elbows on his knees, and took another drink before lifting his hand and rubbing it over his eyes. "Sorry. I didn't mean to bring down the mood."

"You didn't. Besides, I brought it up. Will, I can't help but think there's some survivor's guilt coming into play here. Is it possible?"

"Maybe. I don't know. Charlie had kids. Now they don't have him."

"What about you?"

"What about me?"

"Who do you have?"

"I've got a brother but no one depending on me like Charlie."

"Does that make you question why Charlie was the one who couldn't handle things but you're still here?"

A barely perceptible nod was his answer, his face bunched in a grimace.

"Maybe."

"Well, I think it's safe to say we each have our own strengths and weaknesses. It isn't easy to watch them play out in others, especially in a situation like this, but it's not selfish to keep moving forward with our own lives."

Silence descended around them. Even the croak of frogs and crickets quieted a bit as though giving Charlie a moment of silence.

"Everything okay?" Logan asked as he rejoined them.

"Yeah. Zoey and I were pondering life," Will said.

"She's good like that," Logan said.

He dropped several pieces of chopped wood beside the pit before adding one to the mix. "Did I tell you about her letter campaign?" Logan asked his friend.

Will shook his head.

"I'll admit I overheard a bit of your discussion. It reminded me that after I'd signed up, I got the usual mail and calls from my parents and brother. Then all of a sudden, here comes a mountain of mail. Sometimes a half dozen letters at a time. It was amazing." To her, he said, "You have no idea how much those letters meant to me."

"Really?" she asked, more than a little surprised. She hadn't done anything special. Just written letters, sent cards and goodie boxes. It had seemed like the right thing to do. And it was Logan. She would've done the same for any one of her cousins serving in the military, especially once she'd realized via her studies how badly soldiers needed contact from home. To know they weren't forgotten. That they were thought of and missed.

Logan took his seat and stretched out his long legs.

"Yeah. Zo's letters became so famous the guys teased me about it but, man, did it help when it came to transitioning back. Even though I wasn't in Carolina Cove much over the years, it felt like I was because she'd kept me up to date on everything. Every soldier needs someone like her."

The words warmed her heart and flooded her bloodstream with pleasure. As a psych student, she'd heard and read a lot about the high number of suicides military personnel suffered, and she'd be lying if she said she hadn't consciously tried to make sure Logan never felt alone or think that he had no one to talk to. She'd obviously gone overboard with all of the letters if his comment was anything to go by, but keeping that bond and connection to home and family was so very important.

"So how are you liking the mountains?" Will asked. "I'm assuming you're a beach girl since you're from Carolina Cove?"

Will's question led them to another topic, but she didn't sense he did it out of desperation. Maybe she was wrong, but she felt their chat had reassured him in some ways that he needed. The tension she'd felt riding him had lessened a bit, and she hoped she had helped in some way. "A planned trip would have been better, but I have to admit it is beautiful here. Though being held captive isn't exactly a dream come true."

"Captive?" Will asked, his head turning from her to Logan.

"Zoey doesn't know how to relax and recover. What she calls being a workaholic is putting it mildly," Logan told his friend.

"Excuse me, you're one to talk," she said.

"I know when I need to rest. You fight it tooth and nail."

"Should I go?" Will asked with a grin.

"No," they said in unison, exchanging a glare before shaking their heads at one another.

"Blink twice if you need to escape," Will said with a chuckle.

Logan lifted a single eyebrow high as though daring her to answer.

She reminded herself she was a professional and that, regardless of how she'd come to be atop this mountain, Logan had done what he'd thought was best for her.

Even if he was wrong.

Zoey stared at Logan for a long moment but then rolled her eyes. This was his letter-writing campaign, she realized. His way of making sure she was okay. "I guess since I can't return to work, I might as well stay here."

Logan looked relieved by her acquiescence, and her mind niggled at her to stop complaining.

Logan was a doctor. Maybe he truly saw the burnout she was only just now beginning to recognize and acknowledge?

Doctors did make the worst patients, after all.

She just had to figure out how to get through the week so she could go home with her heart intact since Logan seemed intent on flirting with her. "Just keep checking in," she told Will, holding Logan's gaze. "I may change my mind."

"You got it," Will said.

The endearments, Logan's winks and smiles and lingering glances that dared her subconscious to think there could be more.

Maybe, early on in her career, she might have believed that to be true. But love was a lie—ask any of her patients.

Better still, ask Charlie.

16

The following morning, Michael still wasn't quite sure how he'd managed to convince Gemma to spend her day off with him at the beach, but after showing up at her apartment door, he'd somehow made it happen.

Gemma had packed a cooler for Axl and bagged up the kid's "necessities," and it had taken two trips to the Jeep to get everything loaded. He had no clue how much stuff it took to get a kid ready. Cooler, snacks, car seat, toys, towels, sunshade, chairs... But he'd be the first to admit that hearing Axl's laughter when they'd bounced over the bumpy sand to the south end of the island had been worth every bit of the hassle.

The boy giggled with every rut, and seconds later, Gemma was turned in her seat, phone recording, to capture the moment. The glance she'd sent

Michael left his hands tightening over the steering wheel and excited to see what the day would bring.

Gemma wore a bathing suit beneath a flowy, patterned cover-up and jean shorts that showcased her long legs to perfection. But it was the baseball cap she wore that had him sneaking glances at her, because even in a cap to combat the open-air Jeep, he thought her utterly beautiful.

The best part about going to the north or south end of the island was that they could park and unload at their chosen spot. No making multiple trips between a parking lot a ways away and the beach. While Gemma settled Axl on a beach blanket with some toys, Michael set up chairs and grabbed the bags of towels and sunscreen, leaving the cooler and snacks in the back in easy reach.

He stripped off the sleeveless T-shirt he'd put on with swim trunks and lowered himself onto the sand after snagging a bucket from the pile of toys. He collected water from a tide pool a few feet away and carried it back to have at the ready.

"He's going to love splashing in that," Gemma said, her hand indicating the little pool.

Michael made himself comfortable and leaned back on one elbow. "Hey, Axl, you ever make a dribble castle?"

He dumped handfuls of sand into the tiny blue bucket and then showed the kid how it was done. Building sandcastles was fun but this seemed more on the toddler's level. Just grab some sloppy wet sand and let it dribble.

Watching Michael, Axl's gaze lit up like he'd discovered lost treasure. From then on, the boy was all about it, leaving his beautiful mama free to relax in the sun, which Michael doubted she got to do very often.

She'd removed her cover-up and shorts during their castle building, and Michael found himself struggling to focus on the kid. Gemma Fiore in a bathing suit was a sight to behold. She rocked the modest two-piece suit with her curvy frame. Yet another reason to love living at the beach.

Gemma watched them play for a while and then apparently grew comfortable enough to lower the back of her chair. Her baseball hat read *Mermaid hair, don't care*, and her oversized sunglasses and hoop earrings completed her beach-babe look.

"Stop it," she murmured in a sun-sleepy voice.

"Stop what?" Michael asked.

"Staring at me."

Considering himself busted, he laughed. "Stop noticing and it won't bother you."

A smile formed on her lips.

"Look, I'm sorry if I came off as a jerk," he told her. "Your ex is... a lot."

"Understatement of the century," she said.

"He warned me away from you, you know." Michael regretted voicing the words the moment her head snapped up from the chair and her relaxed body tensed from head to toe.

"He did what?"

Michael raised an eyebrow behind his sunglasses. "You can't be shocked by that considering how the guy acted in the restaurant."

She inhaled and sighed and he couldn't help but notice. Mom bods rocked.

"He has no right. I'll talk to him."

"Don't bother. I doubt he'll listen. And it's not like I plan to heed the warning," Michael added.

Axl stopped dribbling the sand and grabbed his truck. He made an engine sound and then ran it over the smallest pile, laughing when it disintegrated. So that's what they were doing now.

Michael smiled as he watched the kid destroy the dribble castle and knew within a few minutes they'd be rebuilding.

"And why is that?" she asked.

He lifted his head to see her watching him. He wasn't sure what she expected or wanted as an answer. Or what reply he felt comfortable giving. "No one tells me who my... friends can be."

Gemma stared at him a long moment. He could feel her gaze from behind her sunglasses and his, but it didn't dull the intensity. He shouldn't have brought up her ex's comment for a lot of reasons.

"Would you mind watching him for a minute? I'm going to go in."

"Sure thing." Michael watched as she practically shot out of the chair for the water, enjoying the sway of her hips as she walked to the edge. "Axl, help me out here, dude. What's going on with me, huh? Your mama isn't my normal date."

And that's what this was. A date—with a single mom and her son to the beach for the day like all the other families on either side of them enjoying their day.

Michael kept playing with Axl but found himself studying their neighbors. There was a group of guys farther down enjoying a few beers and fishing from shore. They had music blaring and raucous laughter cut through the air every so often. At one point, Michael would've been right there with them. Hanging with his buddies, enjoying himself. But when he glanced back at Axl, Michael realized he had no desire to be on the beach with a group of guys, free to do whatever. He liked their quiet little space by the tide pool, liked Axl's nonsensical chatter as he dribbled sand before rolling a truck over the piles with boyish destructive glee.

Michael's gaze shifted to the woman emerging from the surf like something from a movie. The guys down the way noticed her, too, and Michael stiffened when they all turned to watch her as Gemma made her way back to them.

Michael glared at the guys while Gemma moved

past and on to her chair and the group, spotting Michael and Axl, went back to their day.

Gemma settled in and sunbathed while he continued to play with Axl. His thoughts circled around one very important question, though.

What was he doing?

____

The following morning, Zoey awake to find new clothes sitting on the chair bottom next to the bed. Apparently Will had been running errands for Logan again.

She swung her legs to the floor and sat on the edge of the bed for a moment while her brain woke up. She remembered sitting out by the fire talking to Will last night and how the three of them had finally moved on to happier topics. She and Logan had regaled Will with stories of their childhood and growing up under the Babes' parenting that seemed strict and protective yet always included hefty amounts of mimosas, fruity drinks, and desserts.

She stretched out a hand and pulled the hiking boots from the top, checking the size. Sure enough, they'd fit. There were also socks, T-shirts that wouldn't swamp her smaller frame, along with several pairs of thin leggings.

"You must have gotten through to him," Logan said from the doorway. "He brought them over this morning."

Should she be flattered the man cared enough about her complaining about having no clothes last night that he actually went and purchased them? Or weirded out by the fact he'd bought the right sizes? "I didn't hear him."

"He rode one of his horses over today," Logan said. "I had to check your shoes for the size, but I think those will fit. So what do you think? Are you ready to get moving?"

She blinked up at him and noted the way he stood watching her, arms crossed over his broad chest, muscles on display, and gaze intense.

Her pulse picked up speed, and she felt embarrassed by the fact he was seeing her first thing in the morning with bedhead and all, even though they cousins had had plenty of sleepovers during their younger years. "Um, what do you mean, get moving?"

"I thought we'd take an easy hike. Nothing major. Just something to stretch our legs."

So that's why she suddenly had boots. The two men must've worked out a deal last night. "Is Will joining us?"

Logan's expression visibly tightened at her question, so much so she blinked at his response. But why the look? Wait, was he... jealous? But that couldn't be, because you couldn't be jealous unless you had feelings for someone.

The flood of endearments Logan had called her the last few days came to mind, and she frowned, uneasy with the barrage of questions that quickly followed. She couldn't help but think she was making more of them than he actually meant there to be.

"No, Will isn't joining us. Get dressed. I'll make you some breakfast and we'll head out."

She blinked at the terseness in his tone and watched as his long strides carried him to the kitchen. He looked tense and stiff now, like he was angry?

She grabbed up the clothes and made her way to the bathroom, determined to ignore the fact the pillow next to her had looked slept on. The blankets were still in place over the bed, however, so if he had slept beside her, it was atop the covers.

A quick shower helped to clear the cobwebs from her brain, and she quickly dried and dressed. The T-shirt covered her bum and made her less self-conscious about the fact her short frame showcased every ounce of extra weight she carried.

The boots were next, and while they felt clunky and heavy compared to her flats, she could tell they were good quality.

She wiped the mirror of fog and stared at her bare face and wet hair. Not much she could do there, but she did have some bobby pins in her purse and lip gloss with SPF. She dug around in the bottom for the pins and pulled her hair back from her face in a messy bun then added the lip gloss just to have a bit of color.

She eyed the sling, but since Logan had said she could remove it today, she left it off, determined to have her hands free if she was going to go traipsing about in the woods.

When she emerged from the bathroom, Logan had fixed a couple of sandwiches and drinks and placed them in a backpack cooler. He'd also added sunscreen and a small first-aid kit. Ever the doctor, she mused.

Breakfast consisted of eggs and Canadian bacon, and she'd barely wolfed it down before Logan declared them ready to go. "Aren't you afraid I'll run away?" she asked as they left the porch.

Logan chuckled and shot her a glance that left her struggling to suck in a breath.

"Are you ready to receive your punishment if I have to chase you down?"

Say what? She stumbled over nothing, and Logan quickly caught good her arm to keep her from falling flat on her face.

"Careful. No more injuries," he said. "Or I'll think it's on purpose so I'll keep you here longer."

That tone. The words he used. What the what? "Logan, what's going on?"

"We're hiking. Isn't it obvious?"

"I mean with you," she said, tugging her elbow free of his gentle grip. "With you... talking to me like that."

His fingers stroked down her cheek and she found herself struggling to breathe.

"You don't like it?"

She opened her mouth to answer him but couldn't find the right words. The correct response would be to say no, she absolutely didn't like the change in their dynamic, but when it came time to actually say the words, they wouldn't form.

And what did that mean? That she liked him talking to her that way? Flirting and teasing her?

"Come on, sweetheart. We'll never get to the falls if we don't get moving."

Logan nudged her forward and then took the lead. She forced her feet to move and followed him up a trail leading out of his yard but away from the path to Will's.

They hiked in silence for a long while, but then Logan began pointing out things for her to see. A woodpecker working on stashing acorns in a tree for winter, the rapid pecking sounding musical as he formed the perfect spot. Too loose and the nut would fall out or a competitor might take it.

A few steps more and Logan stilled again, this

time wrapping an arm around her shoulders and lifting his other hand to point out a bald eagle flying overhead.

With every step, they wound deeper into the darkness of the woods and the canopy of green, but the path remained visible, a sign it was well used over the years.

As the wind blew, the treetops parted like synchronized dancers. Shafts of sunlight appeared and then disappeared like the sway of a ballerina's skirt or a magic trick to highlight areas Zoey might not have noticed otherwise.

She'd never been much of a hiker, but the walk was an easy one as it wasn't as steep as it could have been. She loved the peacefulness of it once they got into it, and since Logan didn't speak again, other than to tell her to watch her step at various places and stretch back a hand to tug her upward when they had to move over something, she could feel the tension in her body slowly melting away.

She made a mental note to make sure her patients explored nature and grounded themselves.

An hour or so in, Logan called for a break, and she watched as he checked out a fallen log before waving her over to sit.

"You should eat," he said. "And drink some water to stay hydrated."

"I'm fine." She hadn't meant to snap the words but they emerged sounding sharp and angry. She couldn't help it, though. Now that they weren't moving through the woods and they had to interact, she couldn't help but be confused by Logan's continually surprising behavior. She didn't know what to make of it. Why toy with her this way? Didn't he know how awkward things would be if they crossed the line into more than friends? Did he really want that?

"Drink," he said, shoving a container of water in her direction. "Doctor's orders."

"You are way too bossy, you know that?"

"I'm bossy because I care about you. I don't want you passing out on me, or have you forgotten you're still recovering?"

"I haven't forgotten, but if it is such a big deal, then why bring me out here? You're the one who keeps saying I should rest and take it easy."

"Is that a hint you'd like me to carry you, Zo?"

"What? No."

"Then drink."

Anger bubbling, she carried the container to her lips and took a long drink. "Satisfied?" she asked once she'd finished.

"Not by a long shot."

She blinked at his words, again wondering if she was reading far more into them than he meant there to be. Maybe that concussion had scrambled her brains a little more than she'd realized?

"How's the soreness?" he asked.

She frowned when she realized she actually couldn't feel any soreness from her fall at the hospital. The slow pace and gentle incline had seemed to work the last of it out of her system. At least for now. "Fine. Better," she admitted reluctantly.

She fastened the lid of the water and tossed it in his direction before getting up and moving on up the path. She heard Logan muttering behind her but didn't pause or look back. His long legs would catch up with her short strides in no time.

She'd gone a few more feet when the air filled with the pungent scent of cucumbers. She stopped instantly, heart suddenly pounding in her chest as she searched the ground.

"Zo?"

"Copperhead," she whispered softly.

"I smell it. Don't move."

"I don't see it." Living in North Carolina, she'd learned at an early age that the sudden scent of cucumbers meant a copperhead was nearby. That the scent was a defense mechanism meaning she'd startled it and invaded its territory. But where was it? Which direction should she move?

A large hand slid around her waist and she jumped.

"Shh. I see it. One o'clock under the scrub brush."

Her gaze shifted to that direction and she swallowed hard. "Oh, that's a big one."

Logan's entire arm wrapped around her waist and tightened.

"Don't fight me," he said as he lifted her up and took a slow step back. Then another. "Keep watching and tell me if he moves."

She held on to Logan's rock-solid arm as he carried her back and in a wide circle in the direction they were originally heading. The snake stayed put, its beady eyes on them, and once they were far enough away, she felt herself go limp with shaky relief.

Logan's response was to swing her legs up and carry her like he had the night of the incident.

"I can walk."

"I feel you shaking."

"That snake was huge."

He hiked her higher against him and then turned with a rough sound of frustration, shifting her and pressing her back against a tree. His mouth covered hers and she released a startled shriek as he claimed possession.

Logan kissed her. Really kissed her. Like a man who wanted a woman and...

"Twice," he muttered against her lips before kissing her again. "Twice I've almost lost you before I've even been able to claim you." He pressed another rough kiss to her lips, then another. "I'm done with that."

Wait, had he said... "Claim me?" she gasped. She

wasn't a hard-core feminist but no man was going to—

His lips cut off her thoughts and took the sting out of his words, but they didn't calm her racing heart or the breathlessness resulting from them.

He cushioned her head with his forearm and continued to press his lips to hers, muttering words she wasn't sure she heard correctly. Things like *waited forever* and *finally kiss you* and *you're so beautiful.*

But surely that was her brain gone awry? The snake had obviously bitten her and this was her poisoned imaginings. Venom-created craziness that made her think Logan kissed her and said those words. It had to be. She was dying. That was the only answer.

After a long time and too many mind-altering kisses to count, Logan lifted his head and rested his forehead against hers. She gripped his insanely muscled arms and felt the ragged intake of his breaths.

"Come on. We need to have a talk and this isn't the place to do it."

She blinked and tried to regain her senses as her mind jumbled with questions and... thoughts of what had just happened. The feel of him, the scent of him, the things he'd said. A rushing sound created more havoc as she struggled to focus. To find the source of pain from the snake bite she didn't feel but knew had to be there.

"Zoey," he said, his voice firmer than before. "It's not much farther now. Do I need to carry you?"

"Am I dying? Did it bite me?"

She stared down at her feet, looking for a sign of the snake's strike. She hadn't really thought about dying, but she supposed a beautiful trail in the deep woods wasn't the worst way to go. It was better than being in a hospital hooked up to machines that bleeped and having people poke and prod you nonstop.

And then there was Logan and his kisses. They were really good kisses.

"Breathe, Zoey," Logan ordered. "Are you panicking because I kissed you?"

18

She wasn't panicking. Was she? Could that be why she couldn't breathe?

"Zoey, you aren't dying. The snake didn't bite you."

Her voice shook when she spoke. "But you just... you kissed me. Like, a lot."

Logan muttered something under his breath, and her world spun as he lifted her into his arms and charged through the woods like a man possessed, though she supposed, for him, he merely walked, and this was what it was like to actually have long legs. His stride was more than double hers, so it felt like they rushed, especially given the walk-created breeze hitting her hot face.

Zoey stared up at Logan but he didn't make eye contact. The jostling went on as his long legs ate up the distance, and then the world spun again when he broke through a clearing from the brush and trees, and he lowered her onto a large rock.

The rushing sound was so loud now that she figured her time had to be up. Or close to it. "Tell Mama I love her."

"For the love of... You're not dying," Logan muttered, his tone sounding more than a bit exasperated. And maybe amused?

"I suppose this is what I get for waiting so long to kiss you, but rest assured it won't be long until I do it again."

His words echoed in her head, and when she finally managed to tear her gaze off of Logan, she looked around and realized they'd made it to his waterfall. That was the noise. The rushing noise she'd thought in her panicked state was the venom sliding through her veins.

Zoey sucked in a breath at the beautiful sight. It was like... a mirage or something. Like walking into an illusion or that CGI stuff they used in the movies. So lush and beautiful and serene that it didn't seem real. Couldn't possibly be real.

The mountain jutted higher into the sky around them, and water blasted down from the top. The mist created a rainbow in the air, and she wondered how on earth this spot wasn't a tourist attraction. "How did you find this place?"

"The old man who owned the place kept it secret. Said it was his wife's favorite spot. She was a painter, an artist like Isabel," he said, mentioning one of their "cousins." "He was a patient I cared for. We'd talked a lot about me wanting to find a place in the mountains. He sold it to me for a beer, a cigarette, and a trip to the hospital roof for two hours to see the sunset before he passed."

"Oh, Logan."

"The day I followed the trail, I knew why he didn't want it sold publicly. He'd said it was special, which is why this is where I should've kissed you for the first time," he added. "Here. Not against a tree after a near miss with a snake that freaked you out so much you thought you were dying."

"I really hate snakes," she murmured, unable to process all the things running through her head. "I thought... maybe it was so fast I missed it."

Logan's chuckle filled her ears and brought a flush of warmth to her already hot face. Okay, so maybe she had gone a little wonky due to the stress of the moment, but why else would Logan kiss her? Had he actually meant to?

With the fresh air and sunlight and the mist lightly hitting her face, Zoey's senses slowly returned, but clarity remained elusive. He'd kissed her over and over again.

Shock flashed through her once again and her pulse picked up speed. What was happening? Logan had flirted a bit the last few days, and yeah, he'd made a few comments that made her think things that weren't as balanced as far as their teenage pact was concerned.

But was he really doing this? When had things changed?

"I can practically hear your mind cranking," Logan said as moved to stand in front of her. "So how about we get this said and you hear the truth rather than whatever other weird ideas your mind comes up with?"

A huff left her and she tried to scramble off of the large rock, but he wouldn't let her. Logan placed his hands on either side of her hips and pinned her in, even though he didn't touch her. "That was a really big snake," she said, hearing how defensive she sounded but unable to do anything about it. "Someone would be crazy not to panic at least a little and... it was the only reason I could come up with for why you're acting so... so..."

"Interested in you?" Logan finished for her.

He lowered his head until his nose almost touched hers and stared into her eyes like he attempted to search her soul. And maybe he was. At this point, she wasn't sure what he was doing or why he was doing it to her. "Logan, this is getting odd."

"Odd. Really?"

"What would you call it?"

"I guess I've hinted several times and flirted with you but not actually come right out and said it. I'll own that. I know to be direct with you from now on.

So here I go. Zoey, I want you and I'm making it clear right now that I want more than friendship with you."

The rushing of the water filled her head once more as she tried to comprehend what he'd just said. "Since when?"

His laugh hit her face and blew the sweaty tendril off her cheek. He reached up and tucked it behind her ear.

"Since forever. I really don't remember a time when I didn't want you."

"Oh."

"Yeah," he said in mild agreement. "Zo, I want to see where we could go with this. I've liked you for as long as I can remember, crushed on you since we were kids, and I get that Devon and Oz's breakup did a number on all of us, which is why you made that stupid pact, but we aren't kids anymore."

Wow. Okay, so they were apparently going there, to that place of no return. "You weren't here, though. You didn't see it," she said. "I told you about it in my letters and emails, but that's not the same as experiencing it firsthand."

"If they can get over it, why can't you?"

A huff left her, disbelief leaving her struggling to form words. "I don't know what to say to you. I never expected this to be… a thing."

"Bull," he said softly.

He held her gaze and she couldn't look away no matter how much she wanted to.

"Don't lie to me, Zo. You've avoided this like you've avoided me this last year or so since I've returned."

"I thought when you asked me out it was about work."

"If you truly believed that, you wouldn't have hesitated to meet with me."

She sucked in a breath and chewed her lower lip. Okay, so maybe that was true. "Logan... don't you see? There's just too much at risk here. We can't do this."

He leaned closer if that was possible, his gaze lowering to the lip she worried between her teeth until he brushed his lips lightly against hers.

"There is a lot at stake."

His husky agreement had her toes curling in her new boots, and she swallowed hard in an effort to make herself focus. "So why are you doing this? Why are you risking us by kissing me and pushing for it to be more?" she asked. "Our friendship is solid and good. Perfect. Why mess it up?"

"What if what we have could be even better?" he asked her. "Isn't friendship the best foundation for a relationship? We certainly have that."

She squeezed her eyes tight because of the hope and surge of want that spread through her chest at his words. "Maybe we'd work for a while but the reality is it won't last."

"Says who?"

"Says everyone. Says studies and life and people and my patients. They're certainly proof enough."

Logan pressed his forehead to hers, and she blinked up at him and watched as he pondered whatever he was about to say next. "You're scared. I get it. But I don't agree."

"It's not entirely up to you, now is it?"

"Sweetheart, I get that this is tricky, but you haven't shoved me away during any of those kisses."

"I... I didn't..." She faltered, unable to find her words. Unable to think to even form them. Because he was right. She hadn't pushed him away. She'd frozen at first and then kissed him back?

"I'm not asking you to marry me tomorrow, Zo. I'm asking for a chance to see where this could go, because I believe it could work if you'd just give us a chance."

"It's not a good idea, Logan."

"Because there's a risk of it not working, you won't even try? Really? You've never struck me as being cowardly."

The words wounded but what did she expect? Logan sounded angry. Or was it disappointed? Either way, the tone was there and she identified it because she felt it herself. In herself.

As a counselor, she'd seen and heard it all. And

she was tired. So tired of everyone's expectations that to counsel others she had to have her own life together and running on an even keel.

Because she didn't. She wasn't perfect and really wanted to shake her fist and demand to know when grace would come into play for her. When would she be allowed to make a mistake without being judged by the masses? All because they came to her to talk about their mistakes, she wasn't allowed to make them.

It was like she had to maintain a higher level of functionality and perfectionism. She didn't dare screw up or take risks, because if something happened, it meant she wasn't perfect. Wasn't someone who could help others. Even though helping others with their problems and emotions had come easily to her most of her life, but helping herself? It hit differently.

Why couldn't Logan understand that? "Logan, I had a close call at the hospital and earlier with the snake but... I think you're letting your fear of what almost happened influence your emotions and thinking right now."

"You do, do you?" he muttered. "Is that your professional opinion?"

"Yes. Logan, come on. You don't see that happening?" she asked, unable to keep the incredulity out of her tone. "You saw me hurt and bleeding, in danger, and then the snake..." She placed a hand over her heart. "I appreciate that you care for me and my safety, but please don't think that concern for me is more than what it is."

"I know what I want, sweetheart."

"This all came out of the blue! You've never said a word about me or us until this week."

"I kept my mouth shut because I knew military life wasn't ideal for families. Because I didn't want to take you away from our family and then leave you alone on some base somewhere. But now? I'm here and I'm ready for what comes next. The only thing this week has shown me is that it's time to stop waiting and make a move."

"With me?" Again with the shock in her tone. It was just so unfathomable to her when he hadn't said anything before now. How could he just flip a switch and want her? Express the need for more?

"Where's your glass-half-full side, huh, Zoey? Our friendship is solid, which means a relationship could be so much more. Have you ever just once considered that?"

19

She stared up at him in silence. Too overwhelmed to speak because she honestly didn't know what to say.

She stared at him and tried to imagine it.

Maybe they could make a relationship work for a time, but everyone knew, once the honeymoon phase was over, the reality of life set in. Bills and work hours and stress and chores and... all the stuff that made a marriage... and a divorce.

She shook her head and turned away from him, scrambling off the large rock toward the trail that had brought them there.

"What are you so afraid of, Zoey? Look at my parents. How many years they've been together. I'm sure it hasn't been roses and candy but they've made it. They survived. Doesn't that mean anything?"

"It's not the norm, Logan. Just look at Rayna,"

she said, the words hoarse as she referred to his biological aunt. "And what her very lengthy marriage recently did to her."

Zoey referred to the discovery that Rayna had hidden her husband's many affairs over the years until all of Carolina Cove and the world discovered his behavior in a very public way. Because of her husband's deadly car accident, which involved a famous Hollywood star as well, Rayna had gone into a fugue state and lost her memory due to the stress and loss of the facade.

"Fine, let's look at Rayna. She and my uncle stayed in a bad marriage for convenience's sake but what about now? Have you ever seen her happier? She glows with love because Connor has more than made up for the pain my uncle caused her."

Connor was Rayna's... boyfriend or gentleman caller. Whatever old people dating was called. "He has... for now," she said. "But what about when it ends? Where will she be then? Stuck in her head and back in a fugue state? Back on the water kayaking out to sea? She's already had one intense breakdown. What if there's another?"

"What if there's not?"

Logan's gaze sharpened on her and she fought the urge to squirm beneath the intensity.

"Zoey, this would work. You know we would. Are you seriously too scared to even try?"

How could he ask that? She dealt with the pain

of "love" every single day. "Don't 'Zoey' me," she said, straightening her shoulders and forcing herself to lift her chin. "And what if I am afraid? Huh? Rayna was in an extremely fragile state after all that happened and now she's rebounded. The last thing she needs is to get involved with someone and go through it all again."

"She hasn't been in a marriage in years. Theirs ended decades ago. Rayna loves Connor... and Connor loves her."

"For now."

"What do you want? There are no guarantees, but that doesn't mean you just give up hope of ever sharing something special with someone."

She hadn't given up hope. Well, she had... but only in the sense that her guard was up and always would be. She'd read the studies. Marriage benefited men more than women. And when things ended, women suffered financially more than men. The system—life—was rigged and not in a good way when it came to women. She wasn't being feministic, she just stated facts. Scary, heartbreaking, brutally honest facts.

"I don't believe you," he muttered as he closed the distance between them once again. "I don't believe any of this," Logan said. "You are one of the most loving, giving, wonderful people on this planet. Are you telling me you don't believe in love? You don't believe it's real? Worth it?"

She wished he would move away. At least straighten so he wasn't hunched over her with his face so close to hers, where he could see every thought flash over her features.

She could smell the scent of soap and sweat and the fabric conditioner on his clothes. See the tiny lines extending from the corners of his eyes and the way they only made him look better. Aged to perfection, she mused, trying desperately to think of anything else she possibly could except for his questions.

"You're afraid to fall in love, so you've shut yourself down," he said. This time the words were a statement, not a question.

She bristled at the accusation, and immediate denial formed on her lips but remained unsaid. She fisted her hands at her sides and walked away once more.

"Zoey…"

She swung to face him after gaining some breathing room. "What, Logan? What do you want me to say? Because I won't apologize for my beliefs. Obviously we see things very differently," she told him, unable to come right out and deny the accusation even though it was true.

"Are you really so jaded? You want to be alone forever?" he said, his tone pulling at her emotions.

By the time he stopped walking, he stood toe-to-toe once again. She pressed her hands to his muscled shoulders and pushed. Moving Logan was like moving a mountain, and she wound up pushing herself back a step back instead of him. Her hands looked ridiculously small against his well-muscled form, and once she'd backed, she lowered her arms and took another.

"Don't run away from this. From me. Talk to me," he ordered.

"I do not have to defend my decisions to you. If anything, this argument should prove to you that you don't actually know me at all."

"That's not true. You think I don't know who you are after twenty years of letters and emails and phone calls? Texts?"

"Like everyone, Logan, you saw what I showed you. Nothing more."

"Fine. You won't defend your decisions, so how about making me understand them instead? Make me see what you see."

She tried to ignore the man watching her every move as she headed toward the stream flowing away from the waterfall. At the edge, she dropped to her knees and ignored the pain of the rocks biting into her knees. "You won't understand."

"Shouldn't I at least get the chance to try?"

She could feel his frustration, the waves rolling off of him like the ripples of water toward the stream's edge. "It's not like I haven't thought this out," she said, glancing over her shoulder to see him staring down at her, hands on his lean hips. "I've looked at this from absolutely every angle. For years," she added.

"Maybe you've thought about it, but you seem to be forgetting that everyone needs love, sweetheart."

"There are all kinds of love. It doesn't have to be romantic." She turned back to the water and let it flow over her fingertips first, then shoved both hands into the cool stream up to her wrists to help with the anxiety shooting through her.

Were they really having this conversation? He'd kissed her, told her he liked her but... how was this suddenly about love? "Love is an illusion. A mirage," she said, staring at her reflection in the water. She saw her image mouthing the words but oddly felt separated from them. "It never lasts, and when it fades away, the length of time doesn't make up for the pain and devastation left behind."

"Zoey, sweetheart. Have you talked to a therapist about this?"

A laugh bubbled out of her, and she reluctantly pulled her hands from the water and rose to her feet to face him. "Logan, I'm hardly the only one who doesn't believe in romantic love. I mean, just look at the other singles in our family unit."

"What about them?" he growled.

"Fine. Take Jack for example. My brother is forty-four years old, never been married, and never had a relationship longer than a year."

"Maybe like me and the military, he knows his job as a bodyguard isn't conducive to having a normal family life."

"Or maybe he's seen so much divorce and dysfunction in the people he's hired to protect from people who supposedly love them that he doesn't believe in it either," she said.

"And Lily?" he asked. "Are you saying that's true of your sister?"

"No, she's actually the opposite and a hopeless romantic, which is why no man ever measures up to her expectations and she winds up miserable and crying on the phone about the continuous cycle of failed attempts to catch herself a man."

Logan stared at her long and hard. Like he tried to see into her soul.

"You've seen the Babes' marriages, and other than Rayna's... they've worked." Logan ran a hand over his head and mussed the longer hair on top.

"Logan, my mother has buried two husbands and divorced another," she said dryly. "I'd hardly call that successful."

"I would," Logan said. "She loved them. All of them. And if I'm not mistaken, she and Bruce have reconnected and are dating again. What about that? They were first loves and that obviously hasn't died despite the years since their divorce."

She leaned her head back on her neck and released a groan of frustration. "Logan, I love my mother. She is a wonderful person, but she is not the type of woman who stays alone long. She needs a man in her life."

"And you don't?" he asked.

"I don't," she repeated softly, giving her head a firm shake. "Not like that."

"I get it, Zo. You're strong and independent, someone who has worked hard to be where you are today. I respect that. But that doesn't mean you don't crave love like the rest of us mere humans. What am I missing here?"

He missed the pain. The horrible, earth-shattering, breath-stealing, unimaginable pain of the person you loved beyond life breaking you. Tearing you down to the point that you sobbed in a stranger's office and never wanted to wake up or get out of bed. Or... turned into Charlie, Will's friend who'd died by suicide because he was unable to cope with his wife's and friend's betrayals. Then there was little Aya, only twelve years old and struggling to find the right kind of love despite her tender age. Day after day, year after year, person after person, she'd heard the stories. Seen the damage. Felt their pain. Maybe she had hardened a bit as a result, but it was a good thing, not a bad one.

"Baby, who hurt you?"

Logan moved to stand in front of her once again and he took her shoulders in his hands. He gripped them lightly but firmly, not allowing her to pull away this time. Her hands met his chest and she felt his warmth. The heat of his body and the strength of muscle and bone.

Who'd hurt her?

Who hadn't?

The hurt had come with every patient, every brokenhearted friend, every story on the news and tidbit of information Rayna and Hadley and Tessa had shared. For years she'd found herself bombarded on all sides by the disaster of love. And to her it just wasn't worth it. "Logan, I'm not who you think I am," she whispered, the words emerging raw and strained. "You need to stop pretending there's something between us and... and move on. Find someone who feels the same way you feel."

Maybe she was stupid or maybe she was letting life rule her instead of her ruling her own life, but it was a scary world out there and anyone who thought otherwise... they were the ones the deluding themselves. The ones in complete denial. Logan included.

In the swipe society of dating apps and hookups, did anyone actually feel love anymore? What happened to the old days where vows were honored?

If she had to guess, the majority of her patients were divorced individuals trying to find themselves again after being hurt so badly. It was sad and painful and not something she ever wanted to experience. Who could blame her for wanting to protect herself?

"I'm not going to drop this, Zoey. I've waited forever to tell you how I feel, and I'm not going to back down just because it scares you."

Without a word, she turned and began walking back to the trail they'd taken from the cabin, stomping to scare away the snakes and wishing it worked as well on Logan.

20

———

That afternoon Logan carried a plate to where Zoey sat on the couch reading one of the books he kept here at the cabin.

The book was Oz's latest thriller, where the worst of society showed itself in the bid to survive a serial killer. Not exactly happy reading material—or one he would've thought she'd enjoy. But then Oz was a friend to all of them, so maybe she was just curious. "You need to eat."

"You need to back off."

He clenched his jaw so tight that pain shot up the side of his head. "Can we talk about this, Zo?"

She shut the book with a snap and glanced up at him.

"We have. We disagree and that's not going to change."

He sat on the edge of the coffee table, elbows on

his knees as he leaned toward her. "What can I do to get you to see this from my point of view?"

"Nothing."

"There's got to be something. Are you worried about what the others will think?"

"No."

"Then what?"

"I don't want to get hurt," she said. "I don't want to hurt you. I don't want... this."

"It didn't feel that way when we kissed." Maybe it was unfair of him to throw her response to his kisses in her face, but he'd do—say—whatever it took to get her to see reason. "If you didn't like me, that would be different, but I know you do."

"Wow. Conceited much?"

"Just being truthful. Which I'm sure you know." He watched her, studied her every shift of expression. Their time at the cabin was drawing to an end, and when he took her back to Wilmington and Carolina Cove, he didn't want to do it without some sign of progress.

"Why is this suddenly so important to you?" she asked.

"Like I said, I've waited a long time. Thought this through."

"Well, it's kind of a surprise for me."

He nodded reluctantly. "I can tell it's more of a surprise for you than I thought it would be."

She shook her head slowly, her eyebrows drawn

tightly over her nose.

"It's a horrible, horrible idea. The odds are not in our favor."

"We can beat the odds."

"That's what everyone thinks in the beginning, Logan. They think their relationship is special, different. Better than their friends'. It's limerence. That first taste of headiness that screws with your brain for a while until you realize what you thought was there really isn't."

"So you're saying I've had limerence for the last ten or fifteen years?"

"Puppy love?"

He shook his head, a wry smile curling his lips. "Try again, sweetheart."

She drew her legs up and wrapped her arms around them. He didn't have to be a shrink to see it for the protective act that it was. Zoey's reaction surprised him. Not because he thought he was all that and she'd jump into his arms but because of her fear.

He settled himself on the couch beside her, placing his hand over her bare feet. They were cold, so he held his hand there to warm them up, his thumb finding and rubbing against the soft under-side of her arch. "I can't remember much before you came along. You—all the cousins—were always there."

"We definitely had wonderful childhoods," she

murmured. "Some of my patients… They amaze me sometimes, to have been through all that they have and still be standing. It's humbling."

He moved his thumb over the arch, back and forth, pressing gently. "You've seen and heard a lot over the years. I hadn't considered that and how it would impact things when I thought about telling you how I felt."

"Well, now you know."

"Sweetheart, their lives aren't yours. Their problems and histories aren't yours."

"I know that."

"So why are you willing to shut yourself down out of fear because of it? I don't understand that."

She withdrew her foot from his hold and swung her feet to the floor to stand as though desperate to escape him.

"You don't have to understand it, Logan. But you do have to accept it."

MICHAEL LEANED back in his beach chair with a sigh of contentment.

Axl had played himself to sleep. Literally. The kid had been sitting on the edge of the tide pool with his toys when he couldn't keep his eyes open any longer. He'd slumped against Michael's side and now slept beneath the sunshade.

"I have to admit, you're good with him."

He told himself not to take the compliment too much to heart but then shrugged inwardly and grinned. "He's a good kid. You've done well with him."

"As a single mom, you mean?"

"As his mom," he murmured, reaching over to snag her hand off of the armrest of her chair. He carried it to his lips and kissed her knuckles.

He watched as her lips parted and she inhaled, and his fingers tightened over hers.

"Michael..."

He got to his feet and tugged her up to hers. "You need sunscreen."

"Is that your way of getting to touch me?"

He snagged the bottle from the pocket of the chair and handed it to her. "Considering you're doing me first, I guess I should be asking you that."

He dropped to his knees on the blanket spread out on the sand and lowered himself to his stomach, hiding a smile in the material.

It took several long seconds before she knelt beside him and squirted a glob of sunscreen on his skin. "That's cold."

She laughed at his complaint, and he swatted at her, catching a feel of her thigh and hip before letting go and allowing her to rub the lotion into his back. "I'll get my legs. Lie down," he said when she'd smeared it over him.

He sensed Gemma's hesitation, but he rolled to his side to push himself up when she made herself comfortable on the large blanket. She grabbed the ponytail off her neck and back and out of the way while he poured the liquid into his palm and rubbed his hands together to warm it.

He started at her shoulders and felt the tension there. He squeezed gently and then began rubbing the lotion in, adding a few massage moves to the act.

He felt her inhale and hold her breath when he found a few intense spots, but by the time he was done, she was lying limp as a noodle.

"Feel better?"

A low moan was his answer, and he chuckled before leaning over and planting a kiss on the side of her neck. "Go to sleep. I'll keep an eye on Axl if he wakes up."

Gemma had removed her sunglasses when she'd lain down on the blanket, and she opened one eye, giving him a wary look.

"Why are you doing this?"

He stroked his hand over her cheek. "Because I can't seem to help myself."

BY THE TIME they returned to the apartment building, Axl was once again asleep in his car seat and Gemma looked relaxed and tan.

"Good day?" he asked her, glancing over to where she sat in the bucket seat beside him.

"Yeah, thanks. I needed that."

He reached over and grabbed her hand in his, lifting it to his lips. She tasted of salt and suntan lotion. "Me, too."

Traffic sucked as they exited the island along with everyone else heading back to Wilmington or hotels or wherever they'd come from. Michael glanced at his passengers and smiled, wondering what his family or colleagues would say if they could see him now.

"We're not getting anywhere in this," he said after sitting through two green lights. "How about I take you to see something and we let it clear out a bit?"

"Sure," she said.

The moment he had the chance, he took a right and drove them back to the street lining the board-walk. He slowed even more and watched as she stared up at the oceanfront homes.

After going a few blocks, he turned again and parked in the driveway of the house he and Bryson, Hadley's husband, had been renovating.

"Where are we?"

"A project I'm working on," he said simply. "Let's see what the guys have gotten done. I'll get Axl."

Michael unbuckled the entire car seat and hefted

it from the backseat of the open Wrangler, careful not to wake the sleeping boy.

"That's one way to do it," Gemma said with smile.

Michael told her the code to get inside and carried the boy over the threshold and into the home. Like a lot of the newer homes on the island, the lower level was made up of a garage and an efficiency apartment, along with a staircase and elevator.

After checking out the empty space, he invited her to see more and carried the boy upstairs. He gently lowered Axl to the floor. "This is a kitchen, living room, master bedroom, a laundry room, and a bedroom, with a second master, another bedroom, and a sundeck upstairs."

Gemma walked over to the wall of glass windows and stared out at the view of the Atlantic.

"This is gorgeous. You designed it?"

He moved to where she stood and gently placed his hands on her shoulders. "I did."

She turned at his tone and stared up at him, a quizzical expression on her face.

"You don't sound pleased. Why is that?"

He pressed a kiss to her forehead and led her over to the table with the plans. "Because something is missing. Want to take a look and figure out what it is? I've stared at these so long I can't see it."

She turned and studied the room.

"Bedrooms are off the kitchen, down that way," he said, pointing. "Staircase is there, too. Wander around if you like. I'll stay with Axl."

She bit her lower lip and took off with a hop in her step.

"I love looking at houses. Usually I can only look online, though. This is the kitchen?"

Since there weren't any cabinets yet, the question was legit. "Yes."

The chef in her melted in front of his eyes.

"Wow. I can't imagine cooking with that view. This will be awesome."

He moved toward her. "How would you lay it out?"

She looked surprised by his question.

"Hasn't that already been done?"

"It has, but if you've got a better idea, we can always try to incorporate it and change it."

"Oh. Okay. Um… Well, I wouldn't want my back to the windows while I'm cooking and prepping. So maybe a super-large island here with a stove top," she said, moving a few feet away from the wall and spreading her arms wide. "At least one composting bin and trash here so you don't spill it walking across the floor."

He grinned at her enthusiasm over a composting bin. It was adorable. "Go on."

Michael moved back to the plans and found a pencil to mark a few of the changes she mentioned.

Other than the stove top, the big items were placed correctly in her design. It became a matter of chef's preference for how to set up a functional kitchen while maintaining the beauty of the design. He liked it.

While he penciled in a few notes for Bryson, he heard Gemma moving through the house. She'd found the master when he caught up to her, and she stared at the drawings taped to the workbench in there. "What about here?" he asked.

She shook her head and gave him a smile that made him fight the urge to kiss her.

"It's perfect. This is going to be so gorgeous. I can't believe you do this for a living. How fun."

"Fun and problematic. No one likes it when a project is progressing and suddenly someone wants to make changes."

"So why are you making notes?" she asked.

He grinned. "Bryson needs to be hassled every now and again. He'll be fine. Keep going. I want to know your thoughts."

They moved from room to room, and after a quick check on a worn-out Axl still fastened in his car seat and sleeping away, Gemma deemed him safe and fine for a quick trip upstairs to look there.

"So what do you think?" he asked her as they stood on the sundeck.

"Nothing is wrong with this house. It's perfect. Why do you think something is missing?"

He shrugged his shoulders. "Gut feeling. Something feels off."

"Mmmm. Not to me. Though I guess since you're the architect you'd know."

They made their way back inside and down the stairs. Axl slept on, completely out after his busy playday at the beach.

"What if they have a pet?" Gemma suddenly asked. "With all of the bedrooms, what if a family lives here with kids? They'd probably have a pet. It would be cute to have a doghouse under the stairs or something. Just for it."

He chuckled at the idea. He'd never created a doghouse before, but he had seen quite a few upscale homes now featuring special places for cherished pets. It was something to consider. "I'll see what I can come up with."

She grinned at him and he couldn't stand it any longer. Michael closed the distance between them, gently tilted her head a little more to get under the bill of her cap, and pressed his lips to hers.

One kiss became two and he tugged her closer, wrapping his arms around her and relishing the feel of her against him. She tasted sweet, like the fruit they'd eaten earlier on the beach, and before the kisses ended, they both breathed heavily. One step at a time, he reminded himself. "Come on. Let's get you two home."

21

———

The remainder of the week passed far too quickly in Logan's estimation. It was only a couple of days, but they flew by since Zoey had retreated behind her protective shell and answered his questions with toneless responses.

On their last morning there, he made breakfast and set hers on the counter before retrieving his plate and coffee and heading outside to the porch.

A few seconds after he'd seated himself, Zoey emerged, carrying hers as well.

"Mind if I join you?"

He indicated the chair next to him with a wave of his hand and fork. "Help yourself."

She sat down but didn't make any attempt to eat.

"Logan, please don't be upset with me."

"Hard not to be, sweetheart." If he was honest, it

wasn't upset as much as disappointment. He'd looked forward to them being together. And while he'd known it wouldn't be easy, he hadn't expected it to be this difficult. Or for her fear to be so severe. Of all the things that could keep them apart, he hadn't anticipated that, and he wasn't sure how to work around it.

"You're mad at me."

"I guess I am. But I'm mad because you're lying to yourself," he said. "If I couldn't tell you felt the same way about me, it might be different, but I know that's not the case."

"You think that's not the case."

"I know," he repeated. Food forgotten, he stood and leaned his hips against the porch railing, facing her.

"Logan, sharing some... chemistry does not make a relationship."

"We share a heck of a lot more than chemistry."

"It doesn't change how I feel, though. Can't you see that? Can't you at least try to understand that?"

"I see a woman who's so afraid of being hurt she's shut herself away from everything. The thing is, you can't be a good doctor this way. You know that, right? You are shortchanging your patients."

Her sharp inhalation revealed she'd taken the words as an insult but he didn't care. He thought of it as hard truth. One doctor to another. One friend to another.

"That's uncalled for."

"It hurts because it's true. Zo, I get why you've done it. I've known more than a few doctors who shut their emotions down because it's too painful to feel the losses."

"I haven't shut down."

He shook his head, barely able to contain his frustration. "Look, I hear enough of my patients' issues from a physical standpoint, but when all you deal with day in and day out is their emotional problems... it's not healthy for you."

"I'm fine," she said, her tone tense and defensive.

"Zo, you are a long way from fine. You're burnt out, and even if you can't see it or aren't willing to acknowledge it, there's a part of you that knows I'm right or you wouldn't be so defensive."

"I'm defensive because I feel like I'm being attacked."

"You're not. I'm concerned and I care. I want to help you."

"And I appreciate that but I'm okay. The best way you can help me is to accept my decisions on this."

He crossed his arms over his chest and tilted his head to one side, looking at the woman he loved more than he'd ever thought possible. Not a crush, not mere interest, but love. "You've buried yourself so deep behind walls you can't even see daylight. You feel safe there but what happens when the walls cave in? When you wake up one day and realize you're truly alone?"

His voice roughened there at the end with those words, and he watched as she swallowed hard and scrambled out of the chair.

"I'll be ready to leave in five minutes."

IT DIDN'T TAKE her five minutes, because once Zoey stalked inside the cabin, she remembered that she'd arrived with nothing but the scrubs she'd changed into at the hospital and her tote bag purse.

Logan entered behind her and found her standing in the middle of the cabin floor, frozen in place due to doubt and fear and all of the other things that came with wondering if he could be right. "Where's"—she had to stop and clear her throat—"my phone and wallet?"

Without a word, Logan moved to the mantel and lifted the top. She gasped at the hidden storage. "It's been there the entire time?"

He handed them over and she tossed the wallet toward the tote bag on the side table by the couch and turned on her phone. Amazingly enough, it still had a small percentage of battery life, and she saw a slew of texts and missed calls from her mom and siblings, the cousins. But none from work?

"I let everyone know you're safe," Logan said.

"But once the media caught wind of what happened at the hospital, they were still concerned."

"And yet you didn't let them talk to me."

"I knew you'd hatch a plan to try to get back," he said, his tone dark. "You needed time to recover—which they understood."

She refused to acknowledge the fact that at least in that he was right. In the time she'd spent at the cabin, she could tell her body had rested and let go of the panic she'd gone into at the hospital. She'd slept. Maybe more than she had in months. Walking the trail and swinging in the hammock, sitting on the porch listening to the birds and bugs and the wind in the trees had helped, too. He'd forced her to unplug, and even though she hated that he'd been right to do so, she'd be lying if she said it hadn't helped her.

She stood there and opened the texts, reading one after another.

I saw what happened on the news. I'm so very glad you're safe. Rest and heal and let Logan take care of you, texted her mother. *See you when you get back. I have good news to share!*

Zo! What on earth! I know you're okay because you're with Logan, but dang, girl. That was close. Call me as soon as you get back... Her sister, Lily.

Hey, Shortstack. Glad you're safe. Give Logan a hard time just for the heck of it, Michael wrote.

The texts went on and on from nearly every

member of her family and extended family of cousins and the Babes. Reading them filled her heart with love.

Swallowing hard, she grabbed her bag and clenched the phone in her hand. "I'll be on the porch."

She left him to do whatever it was he did when it was time to leave the cabin and settled herself into one of the rockers to read the rest of the text messages. She supposed it would've been faster if she had helped, but in the mood she was in, that wasn't going to happen.

It took Logan a while to get things ready. She heard him handling dishes and trash. Finally he reappeared and carried a large trash bag to the truck, tossing it into the back.

"You need to go to the bathroom before we head out?"

She shook her head, refusing to make eye contact with him after reading Hadley's text.

He kidnapped you? Enjoy EVERY moment. I told you he liked you! You're the perfect couple!

Logan said nothing as he locked the door and checked it one last time, then left the porch once more. She followed him down the steps to the truck and climbed inside, thinking of the moment she'd woken up inside it a week ago after the incident at the hospital.

Where had the week gone? How had so much changed? They'd come here as that weird mix of friends and family. But now?

What were they now that he knew her feelings on love?

22

Logan made the six-hour drive in just over five, a sure sign of how desperate he was to get away from her, she mused.

What was worse, the entire drive was done in silence. Thank God for good radio stations.

Logan turned and she frowned when she realized where he headed. Of course. Her car was still at the hospital. He had remembered she would need it, even if she hadn't.

He drove into the employee lot and wound his way through until pulling into the space opposite her car to park. She stared at the mermaid air freshener hanging from her rearview mirror and inhaled. "Thank you. For everything."

"Yeah. Of course."

"Logan..."

"You should get home, Zo. You've got a few hours

to get things together before you head back to work tomorrow."

She didn't budge. All week she'd wanted to come back to Wilmington. To not be stuck in that cabin with a man who saw through the mask she wore to protect herself. But now she couldn't make herself open the door and take the next step. "Are we okay, Logan?"

His hands tightened on the steering wheel so much that the leather creaked out a complaint. That was a big ol' no. A knot formed in her stomach and grew. She didn't want to hurt him and she most certainly didn't want to lose him. She couldn't. "Logan?"

"I waited a very long time to tell you how I feel," he said, his voice gruff. "To get myself back home and established and to make sure that what I felt was real. It's going to take some time, I guess. But I won't put my life on hold forever."

"What are you saying?"

"I'm saying I love you, Zoey," he said, turning his head to face her.

His gaze held hers and the air froze in her lungs.

"I love you—not like a brother or a cousin but as a man. I want you. I want to be with you and start a future with you, but since you're so sure you have life all figured out and it somehow doesn't include love, I guess I'm going to have to figure out a way to let you go."

She flinched at his words and felt the force of them like a physical blow. A physical loss, like having her heart ripped away from her. "Logan…"

"Go home," he told her. "You want to be alone and safe—go do it. But go knowing you're going to have to do it without me. It has to be."

She trembled from head to toe so badly that it took her two tries to get hold of the door handle and open it. She got out, purse clutched tightly against her chest as though it would somehow catch the pain pouring out of her from his words.

The moment she shut the door, Logan put the truck in reverse and squealed out of the parking lot. She watched him go, frozen in place because of the emptiness leaving her feeling lost and ill at ease. She'd gotten what she wanted. She'd pushed him away and made it clear she wouldn't ever be the woman he wanted. She'd done it and he'd accepted it, though he needed time to process things.

So why did accomplishing her goal now feel so wrong? Like she'd messed up the greatest thing in the world?

She stumbled to her car, the keys in her purse unlocking it when she placed her hand behind the latch. She fell into the seat and shut the door, mindful enough to lower the windows to expel some of the heat trapped inside.

A sob built in her throat but she was too afraid to let it out. If she did, she wouldn't be able to stop.

How could he leave? Just like that?

How could he say all those wonderful things and... Dear God, what had she done?

A loud bang and crumpling sound rattled the earth and air, followed by a blaring horn. The unmistakable sound of a car crash echoed through the garage and tore her attention away from her thoughts—but then just as quickly, her mind filled with an awful possibility. "No. No, no, no."

She grabbed her bag and slung it over her shoulder as she shoved out of the car and started running toward the sound of the horn. She was on the second floor of the parking garage, and as she neared the stairs, she saw exactly what she didn't want to see. Logan's truck flipped on its side in the middle of a busy intersection, the bag of trash from their week at the cabin strewn about like she'd treated his feelings for her.

All she could do was run. Run as fast as she could down the stairs and out of the garage, down the street. People had already started to gather, phones out to record instead of trying to help. A siren sounded behind her. As she neared the truck, she pushed her way through the crowd and saw Logan inside the shattered window. He wasn't moving. "Logan!"

Two men were trying to help but couldn't get through the shattered windshield. A loud roar sounded behind her as the fire department from a block away arrived. Hands tried to pull her back and she fought them. "Logan!"

"Do you know him?" a man asked.

She nodded and sobbed and clutched the firefighter's arm as he tugged her back to allow his buddies access to do their job. What had she done? Logan had given her what she wanted. He'd left her alone. Driven away—and all she wanted now was everything he'd said they could have. "Help him. Please, help him. I love him."

BACK AT HER APARTMENT BUILDING, Gemma carried Axl on her hip while Michael carried the beach supplies behind her up the stairs.

"Thank you for a great day," she said, smiling at him over her shoulder.

"I can't wait to do it again sometime," he said.

It wasn't until they topped the steps and Gemma drew up short that Michael shifted his gaze and spotted her ex standing on her doorstep. Dennis's red face revealed his anger if the fists at his sides weren't enough of a clue.

"Where have you been?" he demanded of Gemma.

"We went to the beach," she said. "Why are you here?"

"It's my weekend."

Gemma huffed and shook her head. "You didn't contact me to make arrangements. I didn't think you were coming. Again," she added.

"So you just take off with my son?"

Axl lifted his sleepy head from his mother's shoulder and stared at the man who'd fathered him.

"Why don't we take this out of the hallway," Gemma said.

She hefted Axl higher on her hip and used her keys to unlock the door. She went in with Axl and Dennis followed her, turning to block the door when Michael attempted to enter as well.

"This is between us," the man growled.

"I'm not leaving them alone with you in a temper. Get over yourself," Michael said, shouldering his way past the man.

Dennis bullied to get his way and Michael wasn't having it. Gemma had enough responsibility to shoulder as a single parent without dealing with her ex's crap.

Michael met Gemma's gaze and she shifted uncomfortably.

"I'm going to put Axl in his room while we talk."

The moment she was out of sight, Dennis straightened.

"I thought I told you to stay away from her."

Michael lowered the beach stuff to the floor to be dealt with later and glared. "Why would you think I'd listen to you?"

"That is my son. Gemma is my—"

"Gemma is nothing to you but your baby mama," Gemma said when she returned to the room. "You made that very clear when you married the woman you cheated on me with."

Dennis swung to face her. "Axl is my son. Mine," he said again. "Since you can't seem to remember that, maybe I should file for custody."

Michael quickly grabbed Gemma, wrapping his arm around her waist when her mama bear kicked in at the threat to her son and she lunged for Dennis. "Leave. Now," Michael ordered the man.

"Don't tell me what to do," Dennis said.

"Leave or I call the cops and press charges for trespassing," Gemma growled.

"Fine. But this isn't over," Dennis said to her. "We'll finish this when your boy toy isn't around. Better yet, that'll be my condition. You don't want me coming after custody, you stay away from him."

Dennis turned on his Italian leather heel and stalked away, slamming his way out of the apartment with all the drama he could create. The noise apparently startled Axl, who wailed from his bedroom.

"I'll get him," Michael said, pulling his arm from her waist.

"No," Gemma said, avoiding his gaze. "Michael, please, you should go."

"Sweetheart, he's bluffing. He's a bully trying to manipulate you so he can control you."

"I know that. But right now it's working because... I can't risk losing my son."

"You won't."

"You don't know that. Dennis married into money and power and connections. Please, Michael, just... leave. I'll text you later."

He didn't like it. He didn't like it at all, because he knew a brush-off when he heard one. He cradled her face in his hands and lowered his head, brushing his lips over hers and lingering over the contact. This wasn't goodbye. It couldn't be. "Baby, don't let him get inside your head."

Gemma nodded once and stole away from him, avoiding eye contact before rushing down the hallway to her son. He watched her go before turning toward the door and letting himself out, careful to lock it behind him in case Dennis returned.

He hesitated before pulling it all the way closed. This was not how he'd expected the wonderful day to end.

23

It was all such a blur.

Zoey wasn't allowed inside the ambulance. Once the doors were about to close and they were ready to transport, she started running for the hospital's emergency entrance and didn't stop until she got there. By then they'd already rolled Logan inside and were disappearing behind double doors when someone on staff stopped her mad rush after him and told her she had to wait.

She'd found her way to a corner of the waiting room and leaned heavily against a support beam, hands trembling uncontrollably as she pulled her phone from her bag. She'd charged it on the way back to Wilmington.

She pulled up Logan's parents' home number but then quickly slid back and chose Michael's cell instead.

"Hey, Shortstack," he said in greeting. "Logan finally let you out of lockup?"

She frowned at the sound of his voice. It sounded tense and strained but that was a question for another time. "He's hurt. They just took him back. We're at the hospital."

"What did you say?" Michael asked. "Where are you?"

She cleared her throat of the lump making her voice thready and weak and tried again. "Logan dropped me off at the hospital. He'd just pulled away when a truck hit him. Michael, you've got to come."

"I'm close by," he said. "I'm on my way. Do my parents know?"

"No, I started to but I-I called you first." Her voice broke on a sob and she heard Michael swear on the other end of the call.

"You're in the ER?"

"Yes," she whispered.

"I'll be there in a few minutes and call them once I get there. Zoey? He'll be okay."

"He didn't look okay." He looked pale and bloody and broken. She knew at least one of his legs had a compound fracture. She'd seen the horrific sight as they'd pulled him from the shattered windshield to keep from having to take him out of the passenger side sticking up in the air.

"Just hang on. I'm almost there."

The call ended and Zoey wrapped her arms

around her stomach to pace the tiny alcove created by the support beam. She couldn't sit there and do nothing. And even though she ought to let the others know what had happened, she felt it best to let Logan's brother do that.

Within minutes the ER doors burst open and she heard her name being called.

Zoey turned and the sight of Logan's identical twin nearly brought her to her knees.

Michael's long strides closed the distance, and he swept her up in his arms, lifting her off her feet. "I told him to leave," she whispered through choked tears. "I sent him away. If I'd been honest with him and told him how I felt, he wouldn't have been hurt. We'd probably still be sitting in that stupid parking lot talking."

Michael squeezed her tighter and set her down on her feet.

"What happened?"

She went over it all again, adding on what witnesses at the scene had said happened since she hadn't seen that herself.

The secured doors opened and one of the doctors stepped through, looking taken aback by the sight of Michael. Zoey introduced them and waited on word.

"He's gone back to surgery. The break to his leg will require some screws to repair but nothing that should cause long-term issues. Otherwise he's bruised and lacerated but we see no signs of internal damage or bleeding. He'll be fine."

Michael pulled out his phone and thanked the doctor at the same time. "I'll let everyone know."

The doctor retreated behind the doors once again, and Zoey made her way to a chair, legs weak and shaking to the point she feared they wouldn't hold her.

Michael called his parents and sent a message to the group chat that included all of the members of their extended family, and within the hour, the waiting room was filled to the brim. A hospital aide came and moved them to a surgical waiting area to free up the ER, and as they walked along the corridor, her mother caught up with Zoey.

As always, Tessa looked ready for whatever life threw at her. Maybe it was all her years as a hairstylist and salon owner, but Zoey tended to think her tall, sleek-looking mother was a knockout for her age. Or maybe it was that she radiated happiness and the fact Jack's father had escorted Tessa to the hospital.

"Something you need to tell me?" her mother asked as she leaned low and kissed Zoey's temple, hugging her from the side as they walked.

Zoey slowed her steps and allowed the others to continue on. Michael had his arm around his mother's shoulders, and Michael and Logan's father walked next to them.

Zoey's mother paused as well, and after a head tilt to Bruce, Jack's dad kept going.

"I know you're worried about Logan but you seem different," her mother stated knowingly. "Did something happen at the cabin?"

Everything had happened at the cabin. But how could she put it into words when she wasn't quite sure she understood it herself? "Logan... said he loves me."

"He finally told you?" her mother said, her tone revealing her excitement. "I didn't think that boy would ever fess up."

"You knew?"

"Honey, we all knew. He hasn't been able to keep his eyes off of you since you were kids, but after everything that happened with Devon and Oz, I think he figured you and he both needed to do some growing up before you could get serious."

"That's what he said—well, that he didn't want to put a wife through military moves only to be deployed and her be alone."

"That sounds like Logan, always thinking of others. Now, what about you? It sounds like this came as a surprise to you. Did you really not see how much he's cared for you all these years?"

She rubbed her hands over her face and shoved her hair back. "No. I don't know. Maybe? I guess maybe I did but I didn't want to acknowledge it."

Her mother took her arm and led Zoey to two chairs hugging a wall outside an empty office.

"Sit down. You look like you're about to fall down."

"I feel it. Logan says I'm burnt out. Or at least I was before he kidnapped me and whisked me away to the mountains."

"Is he right? Are you?"

"Maybe. I mean, the world of mental health has more than enough on its plate at the moment given the state of the world."

"I knew you worked too much. We never see you anymore."

"Mom, I'm fine—well, I'll be fine," she said. "The point is I guess I've been in denial of a lot of things."

"Like Logan. Why wouldn't you want to admit a handsome man cares for you? Are you together now?"

"No, we're not. I told him... I pushed him away. Told him I wouldn't even consider dating him because I-I didn't believe in love."

"Oh, Zoey. You don't really believe that, do you? Why would you say that?"

She explained her thoughts on love and pain and her patients. "And if they're not enough, look at you. And Rayna. Mom, love is scary."

"Yes, it is," Tessa said, laying her left hand over their clasped ones and showing off a sparkling ring on a certain finger of her hand.

"Wait... you're engaged? When did this happen?"

"While you were away. I wanted to wait and talk to you about it when you got back. And now seems to be the perfect time."

Zoey shook her head. "I can't... Mom, Logan's in surgery, and besides, he made it clear he wasn't happy with my response."

"I'd say not. But he's expected to be fine. You, however, are obviously not. Now tell me why you say you don't believe in love."

Zoey shut her eyes to block out the sterile hospital corridor and her mother's beautiful ring that brought a surprising tug of envy to her soul. Her mother had already married three times. Now a fourth? Did it count when it was the same man twice over? "I guess I thought I didn't but... the moment it hit me that Logan walked away and I'd gotten what I thought I wanted..."

"Wait a minute. He did what? What do you mean he walked away? Did you tell him you loved him and he left?"

"No, he told me... but I didn't say it back."

Her mother drew back and straightened, expressions flashing over her face in rapid succession.

"Zoey, honey, I'm not following."

Zoey inhaled and tried to rein in her chaotic thoughts. "Okay, so at the cabin Logan told me he had feelings for me and wanted to be a couple. But I said no because…" It seemed so silly now. Who didn't feel love except for those emotionally incapable of it? Why had she even tried to lie to herself about it? Pretend she didn't care and love him more than a friend would?

"You're afraid."

Zoey nodded. "Love hurts. It's painful and scary and I've seen it destroy so many people. Too many people. People I love, my patients…"

"What about the ones it's healed?" Tessa asked. "Hmm? What about them?"

"You mean you and Bruce?" Zoey asked. "I thought… he wasn't a nice guy. That that was why you divorced him in the first place?"

"Honey, we all have bits and pieces of ourselves that aren't so pretty and nice. When Bruce came back from Vietnam, he was a broken man. He had nightmares and rages and would drink like a fish trying to forget what he'd seen and done over there. I couldn't take it. I had a baby boy to protect, so yes, I divorced him. I knew we would be better off alone than with Bruce."

"And now?"

The most beautiful smile transformed her mother's face, making her look thirty-three instead of sixty-three.

"And now it's many, many years later, and Bruce has healed and overcome, and the boy I loved so very much that I eloped and married him has grown into a man I respect and admire and love more than ever."

Her mother kept her left hand over Zoey's but reached her right hand up to stroke the hair off of Zoey's cheek.

"Zoey, life is nothing without love. Without pain. Because without the pain, we don't appreciate the love and beauty that surrounds us. We don't even see it because we take it for granted."

Tears filled Zoey's eyes and she blinked rapidly to push them away. "I do love him. I can't get the sound of the crash out of my head. I heard it all, even though I couldn't see it, and I knew it was Logan. I... felt it."

"Oh, honey. That's because it's a soul tie and those are so strong. And scary," her mother added. "But if you're lucky enough to experience a true soul tie? You are blessed beyond measure, and the fear and pain love may inadvertently cause you will never outweigh the good."

Her mind reeled at the thought. Could she and Logan have that kind of bond? They weren't teenagers with the first addictive taste of love and lust. They weren't twentysomethings still trying to figure things out. Maybe, because of their ages and all they'd been through, it put them in a better place to survive the chaos? "I'm still scared," she whispered. "What if things go wrong? It's Logan and

Michael and Adaline, and everything would be weird."

Her mother drew Zoey to her, and Zoey leaned against her side, head on her mother's shoulder and forehead against her neck like she'd done as a child.

"Things will go wrong, sweetheart. There will be days when you probably won't be able to stand the sight of your handsome Logan. But you'll still love him and he'll still love you. Imagine what the future will be like if you hold on to that? To have someone by your side to help you take on the world?"

It would be amazing. She wouldn't be lonely and alone because she'd have one of her best friends at her side. "What if it's too late?" Zoey asked, whispering her worst fear. "Mom, I hurt him so badly. You should've seen his face. Why would he believe me now?"

Her mother's body shook with a rumble of laughter.

"I'm quite certain you'll think of some way to convince him."

"But how do I... keep convincing myself that I'm ready for this? Just thinking about it freaks me out. It's overwhelming."

Her mother squeezed her and the scent of her perfume soothed her frazzled nerves.

"That's easy. All you do is remember what it felt like the moment you realized love from the right person doesn't break us, baby, it makes us strong enough to face our fears. That's why you felt that way when he walked away."

It made sense. It made so much sense. But would Logan accept her apology as sincere or one of guilt because of the accident?

24

Once Logan was in the clear and resting comfortably that evening at the hospital, Michael needed some air. He got in his Jeep and began driving aimlessly, his thoughts morbid as he thought of what could have happened to his twin.

He'd heard some of what Tessa and Zoey had discussed outside in the hallway, only because he'd randomly chosen a chair near a doorway before realizing they chatted on the other side.

And even though he hadn't meant to eavesdrop, he couldn't help it. Especially when he realized he needed to apply Tessa's advice to his own life.

He understood Zoey's argument and fear when it came to love and vulnerability. No one wanted to get hurt. But it was in that moment he thought about Gemma and how much she'd been through. No wonder she'd ordered him away. It took a lot of bravery to allow him into her life, her son's life, especially when her ex threatened her and held Michael's presence over her head.

He'd wanted to stay and hold Gemma. Be the shoulder she leaned on. But he didn't have that right when he hadn't made it clear to her where he stood when it came to them as a potential couple. He had to show her. Actions over words.

Maybe it was habit since he could make the drive home in his sleep, but he wound up back on the island. Back at the home that would be his once Bryson finished the build.

He'd omitted his ownership of the house earlier, wanting Gemma to be honest and not hold back her thoughts. She hadn't, and as he let himself back inside and stood over the plans and the notes he'd made of her suggestions earlier, he shook his head when sudden awareness smacked him in the face.

That's what he'd been missing all along. Not the tiny tweaks she'd made to the plans but... the fact it was a huge house without life in it. What would he do rambling about in this thing all alone? Maybe, like Logan, it was time to give up his bachelor days and focus on creating the rest of his life—the best of his life?

This house needed a family and laughter. Kids running up and down the stairs or getting in trouble for playing on the elevator, and the dog chasing them through the house until it hid in the den Gemma had mentioned for under the stairs because the kids had worn it out.

All this time, months and months, he'd stared at these plans, trying to figure out what was missing, and it wasn't an additional room or feature but more. The very essence that made a house a home.

He shoved himself up and away from the plans to turn and study the room, shaking his head. He couldn't not imagine it now. Couldn't see it without Axl's toys scattered across the floor and… Gemma standing at her stove, facing the ocean as she cooked in her chef's kitchen.

But how could he make that happen when she was so scared of her ex following through on her threat he didn't think he'd hear from her again? He'd only known her a week, and maybe it was too soon for thoughts of marriage, but that didn't mean he couldn't declare his intentions, as old-fashioned as it sounded. Gemma deserved that, to know she was a priority and maybe, one day soon, more?

But how could he make her feel safe enough to trust him with the most precious things she possessed? Her son… and her heart?

~

ZOEY REFUSED to leave the hospital even though she still wore one of the oversized T-shirts and leggings provided by Logan via Will.

Everyone had left except for Zoey and gone home to get some sleep before returning early tomorrow morning. She should do the same. Logan wouldn't wake until then. But no matter how many times she considered it, at least long enough to change into decent clothing, she couldn't bring herself to do it.

She walked through the quiet hospital, thoughts inward as she made her way to the cafeteria. She entered and walked to the refrigerated case, knowing she needed to eat something. Yogurt or fruit or... something.

"Dr. Barnes?"

Zoey turned at the sound of her name and spotted Aya's grandmother, Fran, sitting alone at a table. She'd been crying. Heavily. And given the hour of night, Zoey knew that wasn't a good sign. "Fran? Are you all right?" she asked, rushing to the woman's side.

The woman held a picture of Aya in her trembling hands, and Zoey's stomach knotted hard. "Fran? Did something happen to Aya?"

The woman sniffled and sobbed and nodded.

"She tried. Again. She was released on Wednesday and she seemed to be responding to the medication okay. But then after a few days, she snuck and got on her phone and—"

The woman's voice broke with pain and Zoey patted her shoulders and back. "No need to say more."

Undoubtedly Aya had read something from one of her so-called friends that had sent her spiraling again. That or a message from the boy who'd only used her for sex. There were an endless number of triggers when it came to teens.

"What can I do? How do I fix this and make it stop? I can't keep going like this. She can't keep doing this."

No, she couldn't. Neither of them could. But that was the sad reality of mental health and the fact that certain cycles just seemed to repeat themselves. Medication helped for a time. But it didn't take away the pain forever and it didn't fix the problem.

Zoey sat there beside the woman and comforted her as best she could, but her mind drifted to her "retreat" at the cabin in the mountains. She'd faced burnout, but she had to admit Logan was onto something with his nature walks and bird watching and going unplugged. Maybe...maybe that would be something she could try to create for her patients? Make it part of the program or go out on her own and create a retreat type center where patients like Aya or exhausted grandparents like Fran could go and breathe and lose themselves in the beauty of nature. Exercise their bodies while quieting their minds and healing their souls?

Maybe it was a pipe dream in a way, but it was something she decided then and there she needed to at least look into when it came to the future. Not only for herself but for everyone.

"Listen to me blather on. How are you? I heard what happened that night," Fran said. "I'd just left the hospital and made it home when I heard the news. Are you all right?"

Zoey nodded and smiled. "I'm fine. I had a mandatory week off and a friend looked after me."

Fran's gaze held her relief.

"Good for you. You seem... better."

"I am. And hopefully soon Aya will feel better, too."

They chatted for a while, and then Zoey hugged the woman once again and excused herself with the need for coffee and something edible. Once she had that in hand, she made her way back to Logan's room and inside.

He slept on, the monitor beeping steadily in a soothing tone that mended her frazzled nerves. She sipped her coffee and ate the oatmeal cookie she'd settled on, unable to keep her eyes open. As she struggled to get comfortable in the too hard chair, she remembered how Logan had comforted her after her bad dream and they'd cuddled in the bed together.

Logan's tall, broad frame took up most of the hospital bed, but she was small and more than a little desperate to be close to him. To hold him and know he'd lived through the accident. To know he breathed and his heart beat on.

But would she be welcome? After what she'd said, would he even want her there?

25

The next evening, Michael was on his way to the hospital to visit Logan when he took a sudden turn and drove to Logan and Gemma's apartment building instead. He couldn't bring himself to stay away any longer.

Maybe it was the challenge in Gemma's gaze or the way she tilted her head just a bit to the left when she smiled. Or maybe it was because, after hearing Zoey talk about what had happened between her and his brother at his cabin, something inside of him felt compelled to connect with Gemma again even though she'd asked him to leave and said she would text.

She hadn't. He'd spent the entire evening and all day today waiting on that text or phone call.

Now he stood at her door, because when he thought of the future, he pictured Gemma and Axl and whatever else came with them. Even the hassle of her ex.

Michael hated the thought of her doing everything on her own, taking Dennis on alone.

Men shouldn't have babies they weren't willing to raise. Boys needed father figures in their lives.

But until that moment at the house, he hadn't been certain he was prepared to be that person to Axl.

The thought of going all in didn't make him twitch with unease, though. No, it made him smile, and that told him more than anything about the relationship he wanted to have. Because Gemma deserved nothing less. She and Axl deserved a man who'd step up and be there for them. Not toss them aside when something supposedly better came along. That wasn't love. That was manipulation and convenience.

He'd stopped at the corner market, wanting to be prepared. Now he stood outside Gemma's apartment door, a toy truck in one hand and a bouquet of sunflowers in the other. Maybe this wasn't a good idea and he should allow her to come to him, but he knocked anyway.

Michael heard motion on the other side and waited patiently.

Finally the door opened and a short, salt-and-pepper-haired woman stared up at him with Gemma's eye color.

"Lo— Oh. You must be Michael."

"Yes, ma'am," he said with a dip of his head and a smile, certain she'd heard about the identity mix-up and that was why she'd changed course mid-sentence. "I'm here to see Gemma."

"Ikle, Ikle, Ikle!" Axl said from within.

The woman's smile widened and she stepped back, swinging the door wide.

"Yes, I've heard a bit about you, Michael," she said. "Please, come inside."

Axl toddled over toward him as fast as his chubby legs would carry him, and he wrapped his arms around Michael's legs.

"Up!"

Michael handed the older woman the sunflowers and chuckled as he bent down to swoop the boy up in his arms. "Hey, you. It's getting late. What are you still doing up?"

"His mother allowed him to sleep later in the day, so he's fighting his bedtime now."

Axl's attention was focused entirely on the toy truck in Michael's hand, and he held it steady while the kid checked it out. "I thought you might like that. You want to go play with your new toy?"

"Play," the kid repeated, kicking his legs so Michael would put him down.

Back on his feet, the pajama-dressed boy took the truck and toddled over to his toys and began to load the truck bed with building blocks.

"It's sweet of you to bring gifts," the woman said. "I'm Rosa. Rosa Fiore, Gemma's mother."

"Nice to meet you, ma'am."

"And you. It was quite the story she told about leaving Axl with a stranger."

He chuckled at the statement and nodded. "Yes, ma'am. But since I'm Logan's twin, hopefully I'm not too much of a stranger."

"Oh, please, no more ma'am. It makes me feel old. Call me Rosa."

"Rosa," he repeated. "Is Gemma here?"

"She went to work and said she was staying late to have a conversation with... Axl's father," Rosa said with a nod at her grandson.

"I see." Was her jerk of an ex still giving her a hard time? He'd hoped that would blow over, but if Dennis wanted a fight, Michael was prepared to give him one.

Rosa glanced at Axl when he crashed something into the truck.

"My daughter is a hard worker," Rosa said proudly. "She's determined that every penny of child support goes entirely to Axl and his future, but that means working extra hard now just to cover expenses."

He knew what it cost to live in the area. Rent, utilities, and the like. It was even more expensive on the island, and in the last few months, everything had gone up.

"Oh, forgive my manners. Please, have a seat. Would you like something to drink?"

"No, I'm good. Thanks, though. Do you think Gemma will be home soon?" Maybe he should go to the restaurant and make sure she was okay?

Stalking much?

It wasn't stalking as much as... Well, he wasn't sure what it was. He just knew there was something about her that fascinated him and he couldn't help but feel possessive. In a good way, not a stalking way.

"I hope so. I don't like driving home so late."

"I understand. Rosa, I know you don't know me from Adam, but I'd be happy to stay with Axl if you want to go home."

"No, no. I couldn't do that. It wouldn't be right."

He knew she saw him as a stranger and totally understood her hesitation. This wasn't the day and age of leaving your child with anyone you didn't know well, and he could only imagine the woman's reaction to his thoughts regarding her daughter since he'd only known her a week. He'd often heard people say *when you know, you know* and hadn't believed it at the time. But now? He understood. Because he knew. "Would you mind if I wait for Gemma? If it's a problem, I can go to Logan's and hang out there." His visit to the hospital could wait. He'd talked to his mom earlier and she'd said his brother was doing great. Sleeping mostly since the pain meds knocked him out. They'd keep him sedated to keep the pain at bay and give the break time to start mending.

"No, no. You stay. It's nice to have company. Tell me about yourself."

Michael watched as Rosa found an old mason jar from beneath the kitchen sink and filled it with water. She placed the sunflower stems inside and then carefully set it in the center of the counter for Gemma before she returned to the living area, where Axl played. Michael lowered himself to the floor and began stacking blocks with the kid. "What would you like to know?"

"Do you like my daughter, Michael?" Rosa asked.

He blinked and huffed out a laugh. Nothing like the direct approach. "I met Gemma recently, but yeah, I like what I see."

"My Gemma is much more than what you see."

Rosa's tone held a warning note, and Michael was aware he could've worded his response better. So much for impressing Gemma's mom. "I know that, too. What I mean is that I'm just beginning to get to know her but I... hope we can continue."

"You would like to date her?"

"Very much so." The thought of dating Gemma wasn't a hardship. But knowing she was a mother and she worked the way that she did to provide for her child... That was sexy—and to be admired.

Michael stared down at the kid's bowed head and sighed. Why had he fought settling down? He had to think it was because he'd never met a woman who'd remotely made him consider it?

Maybe he and Zoey both needed to learn to open themselves up to what could be. "Gemma intrigues me," he said finally. "She's smart and beautiful, a fantastic chef, and wonderful mother. I... very much want to know more."

"Good women are hard to come by," Rosa said, "but as you just said, my daughter isn't a carefree single."

"I am aware, ma— uh, Rosa."

"Good. Then you know she doesn't need a man trifling with her if he hasn't considered all of the consequences of his actions."

His gaze shifted to Axl as the boy toddled up to Michael and held up his arms to be pulled onto Michael's lap. Axl dragged a blanket with him and the truck he'd just received and settled down with his head against Michael's chest and a thumb in his mouth. "You tired, little man?"

Axl blinked drowsily but didn't respond, not that one was expected.

Michael felt Rosa's gaze as she studied him holding her grandson, and Michael fought the urge to squirm beneath the intensity of her stare. Rosa made him feel like a teenager on a first date meeting the girl's parents for the first time. But despite the fact he and Gemma were both adults, it simply proved a parents' love never lessened. It made him wonder what his own parents would say to him dating a single mom. Probably the same thing as Gemma's mother.

"You are good with him."

"He's a good kid."

"Have you ever dated anyone like Gemma?"

"I haven't dated anyone with a child, no."

"Logan is a nice man, so I'm going to assume you're a nice man, also," Rosa said. "But do not pretend feelings for my daughter if there are none. She has had more than enough hurt in her life already," Rosa said with a pointed look in Axl's direction. "His father has not made life easy for them, and he isn't happy to know of your interest in Gemma."

"I understand."

"Be sure that you do. It isn't only Gemma's heart at stake."

"Rest assured I'm not here to hurt anyone," Michael said, feeling more than a little defensive.

"Clueless men do insensitive things," Rosa said.

Michael nodded his agreement. That he knew. Several of his female cousins had found love in the last year or so, and Michael had watched as the men in their lives navigated the relationships—sometimes not very well.

But it gave him lots to ponder as he waited for Gemma. Because as he sat there and held Axl in his arms until the boy fell asleep, all he could think about was how this would feel coming home to every night.

~

ROSA AND MICHAEL watched television after they'd put Axl to bed, but the moment Gemma came through the door, her mother grabbed her purse and left for home with a breezy goodbye over her shoulder.

"Remember what I said, Michael."

"Yes, ma'am."

Gemma stopped a few steps into the room when she realized he was there, her shoe squeaking on the tile because it was so abrupt.

The moment the door shut behind her mother, Gemma asked, "What are you doing here?"

"I wanted to talk to you," he said, giving her a once-over because he couldn't help himself.

Tonight's outfit was a sleeveless shirt tucked into black leggings and finished off with... combat boots? The sight made him smile and she cleared her throat to regain his attention. "I, uh, brought you flowers and Axl a toy truck."

"You didn't need to do that," she said.

"I wanted to." Michael watched as her gaze shifted to the flowers on the counter and back to him.

"Thanks. But you shouldn't have."

He narrowed his gaze at her tone and wondered at the change. Something to do with her ex, no doubt. "Your mom said you stayed late tonight to talk to your ex. How did that go?"

Gemma clasped her hands in front of her, and Michael moved toward her, not stopping until he took them in his.

"I... quit. The restaurant. I told him I'm tired of him holding me hostage at my job and that I know he and his wife do not want the complications a toddler would bring to their very easy lifestyle and I'd documented his lack of involvement in Axl's life so... he would be hard-pressed to file for full custody, but if he wanted to, I'd be ready."

He tugged her into his arms and held her close, kissing the top of her head. "That took a lot of courage."

"That or stupidity. I mean, I don't have a job. Oh, God," she said with a bit of a wheeze. "I don't have a job."

Michael squeezed her again. "I've got a couple connections, and I know they'd be thrilled to get hold of you. No worries there."

He kissed her head again and then shifted her away enough to slip his hand under her chin, lifting. "You didn't call me."

Gemma's eyebrows pinched over her nose.

"I didn't know what to say. And Dennis is something I had to handle myself."

He stroked his knuckles along her cheek and lowered his head for a slow kiss, lingering over the contact. "Date me. Officially."

She drew back and blinked at him.

"Officially?"

"Exclusively."

"You don't think that's rushing things a bit? You've only known me a little over a week."

"Yeah, but what a week it's been."

Her low, throaty chuckle set his body on fire.

"It definitely has been that."

"So what do you say? Will you go steady with me?" he asked with a grin, smoothing his thumb over her lips.

Her smile transformed her face, changing the worry to happiness and teasing.

"You sure about this? I come with complications. Dennis isn't going to just go away."

"We'll deal with him as we have to but I think you're right. From what you've told me, he doesn't want custody. He just wants to control you and your job and Axl was the way to do it. Now answer my question."

"Excuse me. Bossy much?"

He brushed his lips across hers. "No. Just desperately waiting to kiss my girlfriend like I really want to."

She lifted her arms and wound them around his neck, lifting her chin.

"Well, in that case, yes. I'll go steady," she said with a laugh, giggling as he pressed his lips to hers. By the time he lifted his head, they were both breathing heavily and smiling.

"Gemma..." He rubbed his nose against hers. "We've got this."

The hope in her expression was clouded with doubts and questions and fears born of her past, but that was okay. He'd show her she could count on him. Step up time and again and prove to her who they could be together.

One step at a time.

26

Zoey pressed her nose to the warmth beneath her and sighed, slowly waking enough to realize she'd fallen asleep with her head on the bed near Logan's arm, and at some point, he'd placed his hand on her head.

She blinked again, forcing her tired body back and up even though his hand moved with her. "You're awake," she said. "Why didn't you wake me up?"

"You looked peaceful."

Logan's husky voice sent a shiver of awareness through her, and she told herself to get a grip. After what had happened between them, they had a long way to go before she could allow herself to shiver over him.

After several days post-op, the hospital had

finally released Logan, but that had created another battle of who got to bring him home. His mother had wanted to take Logan to their house, but the Babes and everyone else insisted Adaline and Hubert go on their Alaskan cruise as planned. With so many willing hands around to help, Logan would be well cared for until they got back. Adaline wasn't pleased, but thankfully Hubert was able to convince her to go since they were long past due for an anniversary trip.

"Where am I?"

She grinned at the question and decided a little payback was in order. "My apartment."

"Yours?"

"Consider yourself kidnapped," she told him. "I would've taken you to the cabin but since you have follow-up appointments and start rehab soon, and my apartment was closest and had an elevator for easy access, I won you."

"You won me?"

She tried to straighten again and sit back in the chair pulled up beside the bed, but instead, Logan tugged her onto the bed with him. "You're surprisingly strong for someone who's slept for days." She placed her knee on the bed and then gently settled in beside him. "And, yes, I won you. Your mother had to be forced onto that cruise by your father. He had to pull her out of the room so as to not miss their flight."

Logan chuckled once again and she loved the sound.

"I vaguely remember that."

His gaze sharpened on her and Zoey wondered what else he remembered.

"Did you—"

"Are you hungry? Need a bathroom break?"

"You are not taking me to the bathroom, sweetheart."

"I can help you to the bathroom," she said, cheeks flushing. If they became a couple, became more, that was the type of thing expected, wasn't it? Caring for each other when one was sick—or broken? "Then you can do the rest. Now that you're home, the doctor wants you to get up and move around. Water... you need some water and juice and maybe—"

"You said you loved me."

She'd tried to get up to run some errand for him just to get some breathing room because anxiety had kicked in, but he held her arm and wouldn't let go.

"Zoey?"

"Hmmm?" The murmur sounded odd. High-pitched and awkward. Logan's smile grew wider and wider, and with every centimeter, her fear spiked that the time had finally come for this conversation. Talking and thinking about it and actually having it were very different things.

"I remember," he said.

He tugged harder on her arm until she had to brace her hands on either side of his head to keep from falling atop him.

"You said—"

"I love you." The three words emerged with a choked gasp. "Logan... I'm sorry. I didn't get it. I should've, I know. But I didn't. I was too scared to admit how I felt, even to myself. And then you walked away and it hit me. I felt like someone punched me. I couldn't stand it. I knew I'd made a mistake but you were gone, and then I heard this noise—the crash." Her breath rattled out of her lungs. "I thought I'd lost you and I hated myself for not telling you the truth."

His large hands surrounded her face and brought her up to his mouth, holding her captive.

"You can't take this back, Zoey."

"I know. I don't want to. I love you. I do. I'm just scared."

"That's okay," he murmured. "You can be scared. But we're moving forward, not going back."

Tears burned her eyes and she blinked hard and sniffled. "I don't want to go back. I want you and us a-and more. Everything."

He tugged her to him and kissed her lips, brushing her tears away with his thumbs.

"You would tell me this when I can't chase you down and have my way with you."

A laugh burst out of her and she kissed him

again then nuzzled into his neck with a sigh. "A girl's gotta have some defenses in place, otherwise you'd take full advantage."

"Oh, I'd take advantage, all right," Logan murmured. "Give me a day or two to get my strength back and get used to the crutches, and then it's game on. Your plan to kidnap me has backfired on you, sweetheart."

"How so?"

"Because now that you've moved me in, I'm not going anywhere."

~

Six weeks later

Zoey felt Logan's eyes on her as she made her way down the aisle to the altar. The sand shifted beneath her feet, but she kept her head up and smiled for the photographer snapping away at the end.

She finished her walk, blushing at Logan's predatory wink as she came abreast of him. It was hard to continue. Hard not to throw her arms around his shoulders and kiss him just because she could now that she'd come to terms with the fact love wasn't a weakness but a strength. But since it wasn't their wedding, she supposed it wouldn't be appropriate and she kept going.

Zoey took her place beside her sister, Lily, and

then turned as the music changed. Her brother, Jack, stood tall at their mother's side, and the radiant bride beamed as her son walked her down the aisle to meet Bruce at the beautifully decorated arch.

Eliza Bellefonte-Hayes had done a great job with the decor, every aspect gorgeously designed by the professional event planner. Eliza had built a reputation for herself throughout the state and even nationally, and Zoey couldn't wait to put her talents to use soon herself.

While the minister began the ceremony, Zoey looked down at the ring sparkling on her left ring finger. Logan had gone above and beyond in getting her the perfect engagement ring. The center stone was ocean blue and cushion cut, surrounded by diamonds in a platinum band. The day he'd asked her to marry him, he had surprised her with a trip to the mountains, back to the waterfall and where she'd had to face her insecurities in order to see the love right in front of her.

She felt Logan's gaze on her and looked up, her eyes meeting his where he sat in the second row of family, watching her instead of the happy couple.

Beside Logan, Michael sat with his arm around Gemma's shoulders. Little Axl sat on his mother's lap, content to watch a video on a phone with earphones. They had also recently gotten engaged, and the entire group couldn't get over how quickly the bachelor twins had fallen for the women they loved.

Her mother turned and handed Lily her bridal bouquet in order to take Bruce's hands. Zoey had to admit the man loved her mother. In the last few weeks, they'd spent quite a bit of time together discussing wedding things, sharing dinners, and just hanging out as a group as they tended to do.

Bruce had proven himself to be kind and considerate, compassionate. He wanted her mother to be happy and deferred to her choices, and nothing could dull the sparkle in his gaze when looked at her mother.

Zoey inhaled and sighed but it was a good sigh. Love was scary. It made the strong weak and the weak weaker. It left open wounds and battle scars and more than a few tears. But her mother was right —it also made the pain worth it because love made a person appreciate the good. Had she known before now how much she'd missed out on by being afraid to love...

She'd been wrong about it all, and slowly but surely, she was working on that part of herself so that she could be the best therapist for her patients. To help them see through the pain to what came next. To use it as a stepping-stone to the future.

Logan treated her like a queen but led her like a king. He didn't back down when she gave him a hard time and her fears threatened to overtake her common sense, and he made sure to communicate and listen to her so that he understood. Then, he'd kiss her until her worries were forgotten or at least tempered until her rational mind kicked back in.

He lifted her up emotionally and encouraged her to follow her desire to one day open the type of retreat that was now just a dream but slowly taking shape in her head and on paper. Gemma might cater the meals. And Isabel would hold painting classes. Most of all, people would get the support and help they needed to cope with today's crazy world while unplugging and finding their peace.

One day, she mused.

Her mother and Bruce exchanged vows, and the crowd gathered on the beach cheered at their kiss. The Babes whooped and yelled the loudest, causing Tessa to blush like a schoolgirl.

Since she didn't exactly want to see her mother kissing, Zoey watched the crowd. The smiles—and the pain—on various faces. Being able to read people wasn't always a good thing, and she worried about several of her family members because she sensed their unhappy emotions.

Zoey forced herself to refocus as the happy couple walked back down the aisle. Jack escorted Lily, and Logan quickly stepped up to walk Zoey. His crutches were gone, and though he still limped a bit with his left leg, he was expected to make a full recovery.

"Happy?" Logan asked her as they passed their family and friends in the seats on either side.

Once at the end and off to the side, she turned and faced Logan now that their part in the wedding was done. She gripped her bouquet tight as she wrapped her arms around his neck and stood on her tiptoes to invite his kiss. "The happiest. Kidnapping you was a good idea."

Logan lowered his head and brushed her lips with his, and somewhere behind her, she heard Jack groan.

"I still can't get used to that," her brother grumbled.

Zoey laughed at Jack's words. And then Logan kissed her again.

EPILOGUE & EXCERPT OF SEA VIEW AND SOMETHING NEW

Isn't it funny, she mused, how failure opens one's eyes to true fear?

Sophia Shipley studied the outdoor patio and its well-dressed guests, careful to keep her turbulent thoughts masked behind a ready smile that showed none of the terror coursing through her body like electricity.

She'd left Carolina Cove, North Carolina, for college at eighteen and been on the fast track to success ever since. High school valedictorian, class president, lacrosse captain, cheer captain, and more scholarships than she could count. Her streak continued throughout college and again once she'd joined the workforce, but standing here now, in this moment, weighted with secrets, her spiral into the depths of failure had yet to slow. She'd thought leaving Raleigh in shame was her rock bottom, but now that she was here she realized it was just the start. Her heart raced in her chest, her grip on the champagne glass in her hand turning painful.

Tessa and Bruce Holloway danced, the newly-weds beaming with love and happiness. Sophia's heart squeezed at the sight and loved the fact that, despite their divorce in the 1970s, the couple had found their way back to one another again. Tonight was all about them, as it rightly should be. Which is why she needed to focus on the happy couple and not on the stress making her pulse pound in her ears.

She took another sip of champagne and glanced around the gorgeously decorated patio. The wedding planner had outdone herself. Cheryl Dummit had offered up her gorgeously landscaped yard as the location for the reception, and it looked breathtaking with its soft twinkle lights, candles, and decor.

A gorgeous glittery-gold backdrop took up one side, the perfect spot for guests to perch on a lush cream velvet settee for photos. It was all just... wow. Sophia couldn't imagine pulling together all the little details for something like this, but then again, that's how Eliza Bellefonte-Hayes had earned her reputation as the best wedding planner in the area. Some even said the state and beyond.

"You seem pensive," a voice said from behind her. "Is everything all right, Sophia?"

Sophia turned and sucked in a silent gasp. Barbara Lancaster, business woman of the year too many years to count, stood nearby, a glass of champagne in her hand. "Barbara, hello. It's good to see you."

"You as well. I wondered if you'd...make it back for this event," the older woman said carefully.

Sophia felt the color drain from her face.

She knew. "Barbara, I'm not sure what you've heard but I can assure you, gossip is rarely accurate."

Barbara's gaze narrowed into a shrewd stare and she took a long sip from her glass, staring at Sophia over the rim the entire time. After a moment of silent contemplation and a swallow, Barbara spoke.

"So the rumors are false? You haven't... quit the finance business?"

Sophia battled the hot flush of mortification that threatened to turn her body into lava, and forced her lips into a semblance of a smile. "Well, I suppose they are true then. Yes, I've taken a step back from the industry."

"And your step back has nothing to do with Bernard Pitz?"

Sophia faltered, aware of the tightrope she walked. The non-disclosure agreement was quite specific in terms and one whiff of a breach could land her in jail. "Barbara, you of all people know how it is. The rat race is insane and... after watching my cousins and sister find their significant others, it occurred to me what kind of sacrifices I'd truly have to make and...I'm just no longer sure that's what I want."

Barbara's expression made it clear Sophia could talk until the sun came up but the woman knew the truth. And didn't buy an ounce of Sophia's version of it. "Look, Barbara, the financial community is relatively small and I can only imagine what you've heard but you've been a close family friend all of my life which is why I'm asking you to not say anything to anyone. My parents don't know the details of my resignation and I'd like to keep it that way."

"I understand. But I'll just say this. Thirty-two years ago I worked with Bernie on a project and he was a putz and lech even then—and I wasn't nearly as beautiful as you. I'm sorry it—whatever it was— happened. And that you had to take blame for it."

"Barbara..." Sophia's voice trailed off as she battled the sharp sting of tears. Once again, she forced a smile in response to Barbara's implication.

She could do this. She would do this. Her career in finance might be over for reasons beyond her control but considering the circumstances, however unfair, she'd hold her head high. She chose to look at it as an opportunity to begin anew. To find her second passion and succeed with it. It was all a matter of setting her mind to it. "Tell me— How are you doing? Mama said you might go with the Babes on a Girls' cruise."

Barbara's expression made it clear the change in topic was noted but thankfully the older woman allowed it.

"Perhaps. I haven't decided yet. Will you be in the area long? Perhaps we could have lunch?"

A huff left Sophia's lungs before she could stop it. Literally no one in her family knew of her job loss or situation, yet Barbara had hit on everything Sophia had tried to avoid discussing the evening after her arrival. "I will be, actually. I signed a short-term lease today."

"Here? In Carolina Cove?"

"Yes. My family doesn't know yet," Sophia said, lowering her voice to give weight to the need for privacy. "So again, please, don't mention it?"

If Sophia hadn't known Barbara most of her life she wouldn't have trusted the other woman with the information but it was only a matter of time before she had to come clean with her parents. "It was spur of the moment and I'd like a few days or a week to myself before having to take on everyone's questions. Plus with all of the wedding preparations I didn't want my news to take any of the spotlight away from Tessa. I'm sure you understand."

"That's sweet of you, dear. Though I'm sure Tessa would understand your family's excitement that you're back in town. The Babes must be thrilled."

During the summers of '58 and '59, four of the

prominent Carolina Cove neighbors and friends had given birth to baby girls.

The proud mamas had taken the five girls for daily strolls in their prams—and the locals had nick-named the group the Boardwalk Babes—a name used to this day by the sixty-somethings.

"Though I do wonder how you think you're going to stay in the area under their noses for any length of time and not be discovered," Barbara said.

Sophia laughed and downed the last of her glass before exchanging it for another. "It may be a pipe dream but I'll take whatever time I can get."

"Rest assured your secrets are safe, my dear. It's been lovely talking to you and I do hope you'll be in touch regarding that lunch."

"Of course," Sophia said. "Maybe after I'm... settled." Barbara was sharp as a tack and maybe by then Sophia would have some business ideas to run by her and get her thoughts on.

"Yes, well, I'm going to go say my goodbyes. I have work to do before bed. Oh, I do envy you right now," the woman added. "I can't imagine having free time to sit and ponder life's possibilities."

Sophia forced a light laugh but it held no humor. She watched as Barbara walked away and took a fortifying sip.

Barbara had touched on every secret Sophia carried due to stupidly trusting the wrong individ-ual. And even though she had no one to blame but herself, the thought of starting from scratch scared her to no end. What if she couldn't do it?

"Rumor has it you're out of the game," a deep male voice said. "Yet here you are schmoozing. Looks like the spoiled rich girl didn't learn her lesson."

THAT WAS AN EXCERPT FROM SEA VIEW AND SOMETHING NEW AVAILABLE FOR PRE-ORDER NOW!

SEA VIEW AND SOMETHING NEW

BOOKS ALSO SET IN CAROLINA COVE

CAROLINA COVE SERIES:

- SEASCAPES AND VEGAS MISTAKES
- SEASHELLS AND WEDDING BELLS
- SEA GLASS AND SECOND CHANCES
- SEA BLUE AND LOVING YOU
- SEA VIEW AND SOMETHING NEW

COMING SOON: (LINKS WILL BE UPDATED ASAP)

THE BLACKWELL BROTHERS SERIES:

- BABY BE MINE
- SECOND CHANCE WEDDING
- THE GETAWAY GUY
- OFF-LIMITS LOVE
- FLIRTING WITH FOREVER

MAKE ME A MATCH SERIES:

- ROMANCE RESET
- RULES OF ENGAGEMENT
- THE MATCHMAKER'S SECRET
- PERFECTLY MISMATCHED
- BY THE BOOK

THE SEASIDE SISTERS SERIES:

- THE LAST GOODBYE
- LATTES AND LULLABYES
- MAP OF DREAMS
- WORTH THE RISK
- LOST LOVE FOUND

Want to read other books set in my fictional coastal town of Carolina Cove? Check out the excerpt of THE LAST GOODBYE:

Dominic Dunn hit his turn signal and waited for a family of five to cross the sidewalk before he turned into the Carolina Cove Inn lot and parked, dread filling his stomach. Just the sight of the happy families and tourists wandering the sidewalks, lounging on restaurant patios, and enjoying the lively Saturday night left him angry. He should've ignored the letter. Ignored his next-door neighbor and best friend, ignored his boss and coworkers who said he had to honor Lisa's last request and come here.

"Mister? You gonna get out?"

The boy's voice startled Dominic and he turned to see a kid around eight years old watching him. The salt-air breeze blowing through the open windows of his car brought with it the smell of fried foods from the restaurants nearby, and seagulls squawked as they flew overhead.

"Mister?"

"Yeah," Dominic said, only then realizing he'd pulled into a parking place and was literally sitting there with his foot on the brake as he debated his choices of whether to throw the new car in reverse and floor it to get out of Carolina Cove as quickly as possible... or stay the prepaid two weeks Lisa had booked for him before her death.

"Doesn't look like it. Are you drunk?"

A rough-sounding chuckle left his chest. "Do you get a lot of drunk people here?"

"Sometimes."

"I see. Well, I'm not drunk. Just trying to decide if I want to stay here."

"Oh. You got a reservation?"

Did the kid ever stop asking questions? A memory formed, that of his son, Elijah, at the same age. "Yeah, I do."

"Then why don't you wanna stay?"

Dominic glanced at the clock and noted the time. If he left now, he'd add another six hours to his drive from Atlanta. Not how he wanted to spend what was left of the day. Maybe he should spend the night and head back to Atlanta first thing in the morning? "You've convinced me. I guess I will stay."

"I'll show you the way to the office."

"Do your parents know you're out here near the street? You're awfully young to be wandering about on your own."

The kid's shoulders squared and he lifted his chin to a defiant angle.

"I'm almost ten."

He looked younger, maybe because of his small stature. "Well, almost ten or not, there are a lot of strangers milling around, and it's not safe for kids these days. Are you visiting?" He sounded like an old man talking about "the good old days" but it was true. What kind of parent just let their kid wander the streets in a beach town full of people, some of whom probably waited on the opportunity to grab a kid and head out of town?

"No. I live here. You coming or not?"

The kid had spunk, Dominic had to give him that.

He rolled up the windows of the Porsche 911, killing the powerful engine with another press of a button. He felt a little conspicuous driving the flashy car, but he had to admit he loved the power. Just like

Lisa knew he would.

He opened the door and climbed out of the low vehicle, yet another thing to get used to after driving a family-friendly SUV for so many years.

"Wow. You're tall. My mom is too. I hope I'm tall when I grow up."

Dominic locked the car and fell into step behind the boy. "I see the sign for the office. You can head home if you like."

"No. I need to check in anyway." The kid turned around and walked backward, rolling his eyes in classic kid fashion. "Or my mom will freak out and call the police again."

Again? "Does that happen a lot?"

"Her calling the police or freaking out?"

"Take your pick."

"Yeah."

Yeah to... both? Dom bit back another chuckle. Given the kid's intrepid personality, he probably kept his mom busy.

The kid flipped face-forward and Dom watched as the boy ran up the two steps leading to the office. He yanked open the door.

"Mom! Reservation!"

Dom noted the wide southern porch with its rocking chairs and a few chairs and tables before he followed the kid inside, well able to see why Lisa had liked the inn so much if the porch and office interior were anything by which to judge. It was her style of decorating. Beachy but understated.

The office walls were a soft gray with blue and sand-colored accents. There was a comfortable-looking couch and chair in the waiting area, a rope swing hanging from the ceiling in front of a painted mural of the beach and ocean behind, and on the opposite side, a coffee bar, popcorn machine, and snack area with a couple of parlor-type tables and chairs.

"Mom!"

"Samuel, how many times have I told you? No yelling. Inside voice," a woman stated as she appeared from a hallway behind the chest-high desk.

Dominic stilled, uncomfortable with the stomach-punching fact he found her beautiful. He'd guess her age to be early to mid-thirties, tall like her son said, at around five eight. Her auburn hair was scooped back and held at her nape, but curly tendrils framed her face and highlighted striking eyes that matched the blue of the ocean painting behind the check-in area.

"But, Mom, you have a reservation and sometimes don't hear me."

"A— Oh," she said, locking gazes with Dominic. "Sorry about that. Welcome to Carolina Cove Inn. I'm Ireland Cohen, the manager."

He forced himself to focus on her name rather than her beauty. "Ireland? Like the country?"

"Yes."

"Unusual name."

"Unusual family," she said by way of explanation. She flashed them both a smile. "I hope I didn't keep you waiting too long?"

"Not at all. Samuel kept me company."

"Mom, you should see his cool car! I'll bet it goes really fast. Does it?"

"It does."

"Maybe you'll take me for a ride sometime?"

"Samuel."

"I'm leaving tomorrow."

"Oh."

"And even if he wasn't, Samuel, that's not something you ask our guests. We've talked about this, remember?" the boy's mother said while sliding her son a stern glare.

"Yes, ma'am."

Samuel glanced at Dominic and rolled his eyes, and yet again Dom found himself stifling a chuckle. And wondering at the last time he'd laughed so much in such a short span of time. "Tough break, kid."

"Let's get you checked in. Name?"

"Dominic Dunn."

"Domin—"

His name ended with a gasp and Ireland's eyes filled with tears. She blinked rapidly and managed to keep them from falling, but in that instant, he knew she recognized him—and knew his reason for being there.

CLICK THE LAST GOODBYE TO KEEP READING!

ALSO BY KAY LYONS

MONTANA SECRETS SERIES:

- HEALING HER COWBOY
- IT HAD TO BE YOU
- HERS TO KEEP
- MILLION DOLLAR STANDOFF
- HIS CHRISTMAS WISH
- THEIR SECRET SON

THE SEASIDE SISTERS SERIES:

- THE LAST GOODBYE
- LATTES AND LULLABYES
- MAP OF DREAMS
- WORTH THE RISK
- LOST LOVE FOUND

TAMING THE TULANES SERIES:

- SMALL TOWN SCANDAL
- THEIR SECRET BARGAIN
- CROSSING THE LINE
- THE NANNY'S SECRET
- SOMEONE TO TRUST

THE STONE RIVER SERIES:

- WORTH THE WAIT
- NOT BY SIGHT
- THROUGH THE VALLEY
- LEAD ME NOT
- CHRISTMAS AT HOLLY WOOD
- THEIR CHRISTMAS MIRACLE
- SECOND CHANCES

SMALL TOWN SCANDALS SERIES:

- BRODY'S REDEMPTION
- FALLING FOR HER BOSS
- WITH THIS MAN

SECRET SANTA SERIES:

- SECRET SANTA
- SECRET SANTA II: A CHRISTMAS TO REMEMBER

MAKE ME A MATCH SERIES:

- ROMANCE RESET
- RULES OF ENGAGEMENT
- THE MATCHMAKER'S SECRET
- PERFECTLY MISMATCHED
- BY THE BOOK

CAROLINA COVE SERIES:

- SEASCAPES AND VEGAS MISTAKES
- SEASHELLS AND WEDDING BELLS
- SEA GLASS AND SECOND CHANCES
- SEA BLUE AND LOVING YOU
- SEA VIEW AND SOMETHING NEW

COMING SOON: (LINKS WILL BE UPDATED ASAP)

THE BLACKWELL BROTHERS SERIES:

- BABY BE MINE
- SECOND CHANCE WEDDING
- THE GETAWAY GUY
- OFF-LIMITS LOVE
- FLIRTING WITH FOREVER

ABOUT THE AUTHOR

Kay Lyons always wanted to be a writer, ever since the age of seven or eight when she copied the pictures out of a Charlie Brown book and rewrote the story because she didn't like the plot. Through the years her stories have changed but one characteristic stayed true— they were all romances. Each and every one of her manuscripts included a love story.

Published in 2005 with Harlequin Enterprises, Kay's first release was a national bestseller. Kay has also been a HOLT Medallion, Book Buyers Best and RITA Award nominee. Look for her most recent novels with Kindred Spirits Publishing.

For more information regarding her work, please visit Kay at the following:

www.kaylyonsauthor.com

@KayLyonsAuthor (Twitter)

Kay Lyons Author (Facebook)

Author_Kay_Lyons (Instagram)

Kay Lyons, Author (Pinterest)

Romance Author Kay (TikTok)

SIGN UP FOR KAY'S NEWSLETTER AND RECEIVE UPDATES ON NEW RELEASES, CONTESTS, PRE-RELEASE BOOK INFORMATION, EXCLUSIVES AND MORE!

www.ingramcontent.com/pod-product-compliance
Lightning Source LLC
Chambersburg PA
CBHW011555190726
48287CB00010B/2898